# Christmastime 1941

*A Love Story*

LINDA MAHKOVEC

**Other Books by Linda Mahkovec**

The Dreams of Youth

Seven Tales of Love

The Garden House

*The Christmastime Series*

Christmastime 1939: Prequel to
The Christmastime Series

Christmastime 1940: A Love Story

Christmastime 1942: A Love Story

Christmastime 1943: A Love Story

Christmastime 1944: A Love Story

Christmastime 1945: A Love Story

Christmastime 1941: A Love Story
by Linda Mahkovec

...

Copyright © 2013

ISBN-10:1-946229-06-7
ISBN-13:978-1-946229-06-9

Distributed by Bublish, Inc.

Cover Design by Laura Duffy
© Colin Young/Dreamstime

To my family,
who always make Christmas a
wonderful time of year.
With special thanks to Helen and Jim.

# Chapter 1

Mrs. Murphy, office manager of Drooms and Mason Accounting firm in mid-Manhattan, tidied up at end of day, pleased that she had held the office together so efficiently while Mr. Drooms was away with his fiancée, the lovely widow, Mrs. Hapsey. Like everyone else, Mrs. Murphy was shocked, outraged, by the attack on Pearl Harbor two days ago. And though she was disheartened that the country was now at war, she faced the news as she tended to face everything – with her sleeves rolled up and ready to fight for the side of good. Once, and only once, had she acted with less than heroism in her battles with life, the memory of which still whipped her with shame every time she thought of it. But all that was long ago. She had since made it her habit to live in the moment, to take each day as it came.

She answered the knock at the office door and glanced up at the clock, noting that it was 5:10. A winded messenger leaned against the doorframe, trying to catch his breath. She greeted him with a smile, signed for the envelope, and pressed a tip into his palm. Good service was always to be rewarded. "Thank you, my good man!"

Mr. Mason, her co-worker for nearly two decades, was just finishing up with a report, and raised his head at the end-of-day delivery. Though he had been made a partner the previous year, he had a gentlemanly way of deferring to Mrs. Murphy, both because she was his senior by twenty years, and because his more ponderous personality rather enjoyed her brisk, take-charge attitude.

Mrs. Murphy waved the manila envelope in front of him, with a glint of triumph in her eye. "Just arrived by courier!"

Mason reached for the envelope and read the sender's name with surprise. "I don't know how you do it. I've asked for these files for the past two weeks. You make one phone call and they rush them right over. Well done!" he chuckled lightly. "You run a tight ship, Mrs. Murphy."

"A mere swabber of decks, sir," she answered, with a satisfied smile.

Mason stuffed the envelope into his briefcase, and took his hat and coat from the hall tree. "I'll look at these tonight. Enough for today. Let's lock up."

"I'm all for that," she answered, slipping on her coat. "What a day! Panic and pandemonium! Air raid sirens, people running around the streets shouting that the Germans were upon us!"

As they walked to the elevator, Mrs. Murphy made tiny adjustments to her hat and gloves, as if establishing order again after the chaos of the afternoon. "I'm glad the day is over and they can start to sort out rumor from fact."

Mason pushed the elevator button. "I have to say, those air raid sirens completely unnerved me. I rushed home to find my wife, mother, and sisters in complete control. They had taken the children down to the basement. My mother was reading "Jemima Puddleduck" to the children as they finished their lunch; my wife was rocking the baby to sleep. The only time they appeared to be alarmed was when I ran down the stairs calling out for them like a madman. I felt quite superfluous. Seeing them all so snug and composed, I ate a sandwich, and came back to work." He tried to laugh away his earlier fears, but a note of worry lingered in his voice. "I realized that if we were bombed, there would be no way for me to get home in time. That's a frightening thought."

"You're fortunate to be surrounded by so many capable women," Mrs. Murphy pointed out, in an attempt to allay his fears. She had become acquainted with his family over the years, and wholeheartedly approved of the spunk and spirit of his sisters and mother, and the unflappable serenity of his wife.

"Indeed, I am," said Mason, smiling. The elevator door opened, and he allowed Mrs. Murphy to step in first.

"Good evening, Mr. Grimes," Mrs. Murphy said to the elevator operator, also known as Fifty-Four, the supposed number of facial muscles needed to frown.

"Nothing good about it," he muttered. He closed the inside grill with a clank, sat back on his stool, and moved the lever down.

"Oh, come now, Mr. Grimes. I'm sure you can find *something* good about it," said Mrs. Murphy, who had no patience with complainers. She raised her eyebrows and continued her conversation with Mason. "I suppose if nothing else, the false alarm let us know how unprepared we are. Gives us a chance to set up shelters and stock them with flashlights and food."

"Thank God my sister Edith was at home," said Mason. "She's in between jobs, you know, and rushed to the school to pick up the little ones."

"Edith," said Mrs. Murphy, trying to remember the order of Mason's sisters. "The eldest, I believe."

"Yes. She told me that the school had shut down and that many children were wandering around on their own. Several of the neighbor children arrived home only to find that their parents were not there." He shook his head. "This is all new for us. It will take us a while to learn how to respond."

Fifty-Four chimed in on their conversation. "Starting with proper air raid sirens. Those police car and fire engine sirens blowing in concert don't carry. I couldn't hear them in here. If we were bombed, I'd be the last to know, the last to make it down to the basement. Be bombed to smithereens. Smithereens," he said, opening the elevator doors on reaching the lobby. "This will put a damper on Christmas."

"Not on *my* Christmas," said Mrs. Murphy. She gave him a brisk nod goodnight and stepped out of the elevator, glad to see the elevator doors close behind her.

"Goodness!" she said, shaking off the effects of the drear Fifty-Four. "If the sirens should sound again, I think I'd rather take my chances out on the streets than be cooped up in the basement with the grim Mr. Grimes."

Mr. Mason couldn't agree with her more, but he had a soft spot for the often pilloried Fifty-Four. He winced internally, catching himself using the man's nickname. Mason had a suspicion that the older man's limp came from his service in the Great War, and had perhaps darkened his view on life.

"Indeed," Mason said simply, and changed the subject. "I expect Mr. Drooms will come in tomorrow. What a shame his trip will be cut short."

"They must be so disappointed," said Mrs. Murphy. "They were going to announce their engagement, you know, make a celebration of it."

Mason shook his head. "Hard to believe we're at war. I can't say I'm surprised. I just didn't expect it would start in the Pacific."

"And on a Sunday! The dastardly cowards!" she said.

Mason held the lobby door open for her. "Shall I walk you to the bus stop?"

"No need, thank you. I'm going to do a little holiday shopping for the wee ones. Life goes on, after all." Mrs. Murphy squared her shoulders. "I made it through the last war; I intend to make it through this one as well."

"I dare say you will," said Mason, with all sincerity. "Good night, Mrs. Murphy."

No point in rushing home to an empty apartment, Mrs. Murphy told herself. Might as well make use of the hour or two after work to do a little shopping, just in case the bombs should start dropping and interrupt her Christmas plans. She cast a disapproving glance at the sky, as if daring the Nazis to just try and ruin the holiday.

Though she was by nature careful with her money, her salary increase from the previous year had made a difference in her life, for which she was grateful to Mr. Drooms. She felt freer to buy little things for her nieces and nephews – great-nieces and -nephews to be exact – clothes for school, small indulgences.

She was now on her way to the department store where she had seen an impressive display of toys in the windows for Christmas. The dollhouses in particular had captured her attention – just the thing for her seven-year-old niece. Last year, she had surprised the little girl with a 20-piece tea set packaged in a lovely floral case. Cabbage roses, all little-girl pinks and blues. Mrs. Murphy smiled in remembrance.

She came to a sudden halt, and for one horrified moment tried to remember where the tea set had been made – was it Japan? She stood aghast, and quickly scanned her memory – then breathed a sigh of relief, and continued walking. No – England, thank God. She could see it now: the tiny gold crown on the green swathed velvet inside, and the gold-lettered words, *London, England*.

She crossed over to the department store, and stopped in front of the window display to once again admire the three-storied dollhouse. The tea set would be hard to top, but that blue Victorian dollhouse, complete with window boxes and a widow's watch, would be sure to enchant. She would furnish the house with a few basic pieces of furniture – a dining table, the bedroom set – and perhaps wrap one or two items for the little girl's Christmas stocking. Then throughout the year, she would give various household items on special occasions: on her niece's eighth birthday, and something small for Valentine's Day and Easter – a foot stool for the living room, a butter churn for the kitchen. Perhaps the tooth fairy would even leave a wee garden bench, or a gilded mirror for the parlor. Mrs. Murphy smiled in anticipation at the years of pleasure the dollhouse would bring.

Inside the store, Christmas music filled the air, and shimmering garlands and pine boughs entwined the pillars and decorated the counters. She gave a smile and a nod of approval to the shoppers, pleased to find them in the holiday spirit and not cowed by the news.

She rode the escalator up to the fifth floor, taking in the Christmas decorations on her ascent. A pleasant way to spend an evening, all in all. The North Pole was her destination, where the toys were displayed. She almost clapped her hands in delight at the small stage for Santa Claus, with its backdrop of reindeer flying over a cozy red house with a green arched door, and smoke pouring from the chimney. All along the border of the stage lay drifts of cotton snow and real pine boughs, scenting the entire area with Christmas.

A red and white striped mailbox leaned crookedly near the stage, for children to post their letters to Santa; unless, of course, they were lucky enough to deliver them directly to Santa himself, as was the case tonight.

In the middle of the stage, there sat Santa Claus. His chair was throne-like with a high carved back, and a thick red cushion. A line of eager children, dressed in their holiday best, stood waiting to sit on his lap, ready to convince him that they had been good all year. An elf dressed in green – from pointed cap to turned-up toe – stood at the bottom of the steps that led to the stage, trying to keep the excited children in a neat line.

Mrs. Murphy glanced admiringly at Santa, impressed that the department store had found such a remarkably appropriate man. His beard was obviously real, for one thing. His girth was believable, his laugh was jolly. A few sleigh bells adorned his thick black belt and jangled merrily with each burst of his laughter. He was the *perfect* Santa. When he looked up from his "Ho, Ho, Ho," Mrs. Murphy smiled at him, delighted that he was playing the role with such heart.

Mrs. Murphy enjoyed watching the giggling children, barely able to contain their excitement. The little girl next in line wore a red velvet coat and her hands rested inside an adorable, white fluffy muff. Mrs. Murphy decided on the spot that she would have to find such a muff for her four-year-old niece.

A slight commotion pulled her attention away from the little girl, and over to the boy sitting on Santa's lap. Apparently, Santa was not paying attention as the child read off his long list, and the boy was now raising his voice in an effort to be heard. Santa was leaning forward, his shaggy eyebrows furrowed as he peered in the direction of Mrs. Murphy.

Mrs. Murphy looked around next to her, then behind her to see who Santa was so fixed on. There was no one near her. She realized with a start that he was staring at her! She put a nervous hand to her cheek. What did the man mean? Surely he hadn't mistaken her earlier smile to him. She glanced around at the milling shoppers, hoping that none of them thought she was making eyes at Santa. When she looked up at the stage again, she found that Santa was positively staring now, ignoring the long list of toys the boy loudly read from his letter.

"And I want a sling shot, and a BB gun, and Ma said if I was good I could have a train set, the electric kind, and..."

Not only was Santa not listening to the child, but he now lifted the boy off his lap, and set him aside like a sack of potatoes.

Mrs. Murphy took a few steps back, bumping into a table full of toys, and knocking down a tower of colored blocks. She hurriedly gathered the blocks into a pile, all the while keeping a wary eye on Santa.

"Hey! I wasn't finished!" cried the boy. "I didn't get to the part about the bike. Get back here!" The boy's mother put her hand on her hip at Santa's hasty retreat, and tried to hush her son, who stomped and waved his letter. "But I wasn't finished!" he protested.

The other mothers watched in perplexity as Santa pushed past them and their children, and climbed down the steps from the North Pole. Never taking his piercing blue eyes off Mrs. Murphy.

Realizing that he was headed for her, Mrs. Murphy started to move away. Hurry away. Perhaps he was a madman. Perhaps he somehow knew that she had extra money with her this evening.

She threw a glance over her shoulder, colliding with some shoppers in her haste. "Pardon me. Excuse me. Oh!" she cried. Santa was gaining on her, calling out to her, the bells jingling with each step.

Alarmed now, she hurried down the aisle and crossed to the check-out counter, trying to lose him. Surely one of the salespeople would stop the man, notify security.

"Excuse me, sir." She held up a finger trying to get the attention of one of the harried sales clerks.

"Be right with you ma'am," responded the clerk behind the cash register.

She rapped her knuckles on the glass countertop. "I say! There's a –"

The jingling bells were closer now. She turned around and saw that Santa was coming towards her, moving rather briskly for such a large man.

He waved his hands, calling out, "Wait! Hold on there!"

She bolted from the counter and circled round it, only to find herself back at the North Pole. Where was the escalator? She had lost her bearings in her flight from Santa.

Jingle, jangle.

Another glance over her shoulder. He was on her heels now!

With a sense of fright, she realized that no one was coming to her rescue, and that she must face the deranged Santa on her own. Mrs. Murphy whipped around and braced for some kind of attack or altercation. She held up her purse in front of her chest and gave her fiercest stare, usually reserved for her youngest nephew.

She gasped when Santa ran up next to her, took her arm, and smiled, as if she should be pleased to see him.

"Get your hands off me!" She slapped his hand away and held her purse even tighter and higher.

Santa's happiness left his face and was replaced by disappointment. He took a step back. "Do ye not recognize me, then?"

"I don't care if you're Saint Nicholas or the good angel Gabriel himself, off with you! I've no need of your services!"

A small crowd had gathered, pointing and laughing, entertained by the spectacle.

Finding that Santa posed no immediate threat, and feeling some degree of safety with the crowd now around her, Mrs. Murphy tried to regain her dignity by straightening her shoulders, and smoothing down her coat. She raised her chin and huffed. "I should think my age alone would be protection enough against the likes of you!"

A slow smile spread across Santa's face, and his blue eyes crinkled in amusement. "Sure, ye haven't lost any of your fire, have ye, Mary Margaret?"

Her head jerked back. That voice! She took a step forward and peered closely at Santa. It couldn't be!

Santa took off his red felt hat, as if that would explain everything.

Mrs. Murphy gasped and covered her mouth. And gasped again, making a tiny sound of surprise. Lilting words from her youth appeared on her surprised lips. "Merciful God in heaven! Brendan

Sullivan! Is it really you?" She stared and stared, peering through the layers of forty years, at the young Irishman she had given her heart to.

"Yes. It's me, Mary."

For a moment, she felt a surge of pleasure rising up inside her, and tears started to her eyes, though whether from happiness or pain she didn't have time to consider.

Laughter from the crowd made Mrs. Murphy aware of the ridiculousness of her situation. Her tenderness gave way to a tone of admonishment. "Well, why didn't you say so? Letting me go on making a fool of myself." But now she, too, was laughing, to find herself arguing with Santa, and from the pure delight at seeing Brendan again, after all these years. "My, but it's good to see you!"

The crowd slowly dispersed, having enjoyed the brief drama in the middle of their holiday shopping. A few heads kept turning back to see if there was to be any further development.

Brendan Sullivan took both of Mrs. Murphy's gloved hands and squeezed them. They stood smiling at one another, their eyes briefly scanning the other, before settling into an old familiar eye lock that forty years did nothing to diminish.

Mrs. Murphy was the first to break away, look around, and point to the children, who were calling out, "Santa! Santa! Come back. It's my turn."

Santa sniffed and tried to laugh away his emotion. "I must go. I'll be through in fifteen minutes. Will ye wait for me?"

Mrs. Murphy's cheeks were flushed a warm pink. She squeezed his arm. "Yes, of course! Go, go! You mustn't disappoint the children."

He returned to the North Pole, where the frazzled elf was trying his hardest to re-establish order in the curious children.

Santa climbed the stairs and settled into his cushiony seat, his cheeks redder and his twinkly blue eyes brighter, looking more than ever like a picture-book Santa. He listened to the rest of the children, glancing out again and again, delighted to find Mrs. Murphy chuckling at his playful performance.

He got through the remaining children rather quickly, promising them everything they asked for, to the consternation of a few mothers. But Santa was in his element now. He had the world to give, and wished the best for all these hopeful young children, for everyone!

Mrs. Murphy stood transfixed, suffused with a sensation of life stirring, memories unfurling. There was Brendan. There was his merriment, his barrel chest, the tossing back of his head in laughter. There he was, just as he used to be. A pain deep inside her began to creep over her happiness, shooting its tingling tendrils all through her. Her smile disappeared in tiny increments.

Santa was just agreeing to the wish lists from the last of the children, two bouncing sisters. With bells jangling, he finished with a hearty flourish of "Ho, ho, ho!" He raised his head to once more fill his eyes with Mrs. Murphy – but she was not there.

He shifted in his chair, and scanned the area around him. The last of the mothers led their happy children away. The green-clad elf rested an elbow on the North Pole mailbox, tapping his pointed shoe back and forth to cheery Christmas music, while he chatted with a pretty sales clerk.

Brendan leaned forward, hands on his knees, staring at the empty place where Mrs. Murphy had stood. For a brief moment, he wondered if he had imagined the whole thing, was once again conjuring up images as he used to do.

He climbed down the steps and moved to the spot where he had seen her. "Mary Margaret?" he called out. "Mary!" He looked around. Perhaps she went to the powder room. Perhaps she was making a quick purchase somewhere. He waited a bit, and then walked up and down the aisle.

Then around the entire floor.

Then up and down the escalator, peering out over the store.

For the next half hour, Santa wandered through the department store, talking to himself. "You daft man. Why did you think she would wait? Did you not learn your lesson well enough once?"

# Chapter 2

෨

Lillian Hapsey embraced her sister on the crowded train platform, grateful that, as usual, Annette was strong and in control. Lillian had tried to make the most of their last hours together, but every moment of the day was now darkened. The shadow of war loomed over everything.

"I still can't believe it," said Lillian.

Annette pressed a basket of apple butter and fruit preserves into Lillian's arms. "Neither can I," she said. "At least we had a few days together. And I was finally able to meet Charles, after hearing about him for almost a year."

Lillian's heart filled with tenderness as she watched Charles shake hands with Annette's husband, Bernie. Charles had formed an immediate and comfortable rapport with Annette and Bernie, taking an interest in the details of their orchard, and enjoying the lively discussions they had in the evenings. And he had quickly become "Uncle Charlie" to their three small children, giving them piggy back rides and playing hide-and-seek with them.

Lillian overheard her sons already making plans with their cousins for their next trip. Gabriel, at seven years old, loved having three younger cousins who looked up to him. It was the first time Lillian had ever seen him in an older, protective role, and he had clearly enjoyed the position.

Tommy, on the other hand, didn't want to play with little kids and had complained the whole train ride that there would be no one his own age to pal around with. So when his uncle Bernie announced that his ten-year-old nephew, Danny, the same age as Tommy, was staying with them, Tommy was beside himself with joy. Lillian watched now as Tommy and Danny argued over the merits of the Brooklyn Dodgers versus the Yankees, and made a last minute marble trade.

Annette turned to Charles. "I'm so happy we were able to meet. And I guess we'll see you all in the spring?"

"Soon, I hope," said Charles, lifting the lunch hamper at his feet. "Come on boys, climb aboard."

Tommy and Gabriel scampered up the steps, followed by Lillian and Charles. Lillian turned around to wave goodbye to her sister and family.

Annette gave her a reassuring smile, and walked along the train as it began to pull out. "Remember to stock up on things as soon as you get back. Especially sugar!"

Lillian nodded and gave a final wave, her slender figure in blue hat and coat framed by the train doorway. She tried to put on a cheerful face, but a trace of sadness seeped through as she looked out at her sister and recognized the same expression.

Charles found them seats facing each other and placed their things on the rack above. Tommy managed to open the window a bit, and he and Gabriel called out their final goodbyes. Tommy pointed an imaginary machine gun at Danny and fired a round: "Take that, you dirty Jap!"

Danny spun around in melodramatic death throes, and then ran alongside the train. "See you, Tommy! Bye, Gabriel!"

"Tommy!" scolded Lillian.

"What?" said Tommy, with an exaggerated drop of his mouth. "They bombed us, Mom!" He plopped down in his seat and slouched back. "We barely got here and have to go home already! All because of the dirty Japs. We were supposed to stay ten days," he grumbled. "You said we could help them find a Christmas tree and cut it down. I didn't even get to see the beaver dam Danny found."

"Yeah," said Gabriel. "And we didn't even get to ride the pony."

"It's best we get back home," said Charles. "It might not be so easy to travel in the coming days. We'll come back as soon as we can. Maybe in the summer."

Lillian shot Charles a look of surprise at the word *summer* – their wedding was planned for May at Annette's. Charles folded his coat and stowed it above his seat. He must be preoccupied with everything, she thought. She would be relieved when they were finally married. Right now, her plans with Charles seemed the only stable point amid the turmoil of a changing world.

Lillian was on edge, fearful of what lay ahead. She was frazzled by the last-minute packing and their hasty departure, and disappointed at not being able to spend time with Annette. She had carefully planned the visit months ago, and had so looked forward to her and Charles spending time with Annette and Bernie.

Tommy and Gabriel were standing at the window, but now that the train had picked up speed, they began to fight over who would get the window seat.

"No fighting!" Lillian said, exasperated. "Come take my seat, Gabriel!" She left her window seat and sat in the aisle seat across from Charles.

Gabriel darted into the seat, carrying an old burlap bag with sticks poking out of it. One of the sticks snagged on Lillian's coat sleeve.

"And put that bag of dirty sticks away! I told you to leave it behind." She heard the note of anger in her voice and tried to soften it. "What do you need sticks for anyway?"

"They're for my friend, Tiny."

Tommy rolled his eyes and twirled his finger in "cuckoo" circles by his ear.

Lillian took the bag and shoved it under the seat. "Well, keep them out of the way."

She took a deep breath and looked at Tommy and Gabriel. They seemed all right. At least at this point. For now, war was just a word, an abstraction. An interruption in their plans for playing with their cousins. She hoped they would never experience bombs, and fires, and food shortages, and… She stopped her thoughts, and rested her eyes on Charles. Thank God, she had him. He always seemed so calm, so in control. He would be there to help her.

Charles had purchased the *New York Times* at the station and now opened it, eager to read the latest details. Lillian crossed over to him and sat on the arm rest, her hand on his shoulder. She read the headlines: *U.S. Declares War, Pacific Battle Widens; Manila Area Bombed; 1,500 Dead in Hawaii; Hostile Planes Sighted at San Francisco.*

"Fifteen hundred! So many?" exclaimed Lillian. "My God, planes over San Francisco?" she said, almost in a whisper, afraid of alarming the boys.

Gabriel kicked his feet against his seat while he looked at a photograph on the back of the newspaper. "I want one of those!" he said, pointing.

Lillian leaned around to see the back of the paper. Her brows contracted at the photo, and she gave a low groan. "Hope to God it doesn't come to that." It was a photograph of a group of children somewhere in England, pulling a wagon full of scrap metal. They all appeared happy, smiling at the photographer. Each child had a little cardboard box on a string hanging around their necks, worn like a satchel – across the chest and hanging at the side.

Gabriel sat up and studied the photograph. "Mommy! I want one of those. One of those little boxes. Can I have one?"

Lillian went back to her seat; her eyes sought out help from Charles.

He caught her glance and folded the paper to see what had caught Gabriel's attention. "Those aren't toys, Gabriel," he said. "The boxes contain gas masks."

Gabriel tilted his head in puzzlement.

"In case the enemy uses poison," Charles explained.

Gabriel still looked blank.

"So the children won't breathe it in," Charles continued.

Gabriel jerked his head back, more in surprise than in fear. "You mean they want to poison kids?"

"They want to kill everybody," said Tommy, rummaging around in a bag. "Except themselves."

Gabriel looked to Tommy, and then back to Charles for an answer.

Charles searched for words of explanation for how to make the world sound less like the frightening madhouse it was fast becoming. "It's best to be careful," he said, letting his inadequate words drift off.

"Then I better get one," Gabriel said, closing the matter, and kicking his seat again.

Tommy pulled out a rolled up comic book and tapped Gabriel on the head with it. "Here, Gabe. Danny gave me two of his comics. You can read *Green Hornet*. I'll read *Superman*. Then we'll switch. Don't get it dirty."

The tenseness around Lillian's mouth softened into a smile. It made her happy that Tommy was showing an interest in Gabriel. Lately, he had taken to treating Gabriel like a tag-along, and often shooed him away from his games with the older boys. Though brief, the trip to Annette's had been good for Gabriel; his cousins had followed him around everywhere, making him feel important and wanted.

There were her boys, she thought, gazing at them – Tommy with his stubborn cowlick and sprinkle of freckles across his nose. The all-American boy. Gabriel, with his soft curls and wide eyes, still had the aura of an angel about him. Her boys. So vulnerable, so young. She suddenly put her hands to her mouth and realized that she was scared to death for them. What if they *were* going to need gas masks? Where would the nearest bomb shelter be, if it came to that?

She impulsively leaned over and kissed them. "My darling boys!"

Gabriel looked up and smiled, but Tommy frowned and wiped his cheek where she had kissed him, never taking his eyes off his *Superman* comic book.

Lillian saw that Charles was gently smiling at her. She knew that he understood everything – her fear, her worry, her sadness. Just having him beside her brought a sense of comfort and safety, knowing that she wouldn't have to go through the war on her own. He would be with her. They would be married, a couple. They would be a family.

She looked out the window, clearly remembering the evening before Pearl Harbor. The children were off playing, and the adults lingered over their coffee at the dinner table, discussing the possibility of war. Lillian and Annette believed that war would be averted. Bernie was more skeptical. And Charles had been strangely quiet. As Annette pointed out, all the newspapers stated that there were no new developments towards war; Hitler was occupied with the Russian Front, and the U.S.

was in negotiations with Japan. Lillian had thought that it was all far away and would eventually be worked out. No one wanted war.

Then the news on the following afternoon, Sunday, December 7th. A day she would never forget. That moment was etched in her mind, with odd details still fresh and sharp. She and Annette had been preparing dinner. They had just sent the kids out to the cider house to fetch some apples; Annette was going to make her famous apple crisp for dinner. Lillian stood at the table peeling potatoes, and Annette was at the sink washing vegetables. The mention of the cider house reminded Annette of a Christmas dinner when they were girls, and the two sisters playfully argued over the unusual mashed potatoes, and whose decision it had been to add cider to them.

"I might have been the one to add the cider," said Lillian, "but it was at your suggestion. I remember it clearly. And if I hadn't put in quite so much, they might have tasted all right."

She turned to her sister, waiting for her to object. But Annette had shut off the water and was staring out the window over the sink, leaning forward. Then she walked to the front door, a red and green woven dish towel in her hand, and stepped out on the porch. Lillian could still remember the bang of the storm door closing and the rush of cold air against her legs.

Lillian had followed her onto the porch, shivering in the cold. "What is it, Annette?"

At the end of the lane a pickup truck had stopped. Bernie had been showing Charles around the orchard, but now both men stood next to the truck. The driver was waving his arms, upset about something, and then he sped off, grinding the gears as he left. Bernie turned and ran up the lane. Charles had just stood there, staring at the horizon. Then he slowly walked up the lane. Lillian knew that something was terribly wrong, but couldn't imagine what it could be. Had there been an accident? Did someone need help? Was there a fire somewhere? She eyed the horizon for signs of smoke, then waited for Bernie to tell them what had happened.

She would never forget that image: Bernie in his red and black plaid jacket, running up the lane and onto the porch, a mix of surprise and terror on his face. "We've been attacked! Bombed!" he had cried out, holding Annette by the arm, almost as if hoping she could do something about it.

Then all the overlapping questions from her and Annette: "Who has?" "The Germans?" "Where's Pearl Harbor?" "Are they coming here?" "Go get the children!" Disorientation and gut-clenching fear pulled the ground out from beneath them, making it difficult to think clearly.

Lillian had impulsively dashed out into the snow in her good shoes to gather up the children, fearing that the flying crows overhead were German bombers. When she and the children returned to the house, she found the others gathered around the radio. Bernie sat on the edge of a chair, leaning in as close as possible towards the radio; Annette stood next to him, twisting the red and green dish towel. Charles stood next to the couch, eyes fixed on the radio. The children took their places on the couch, or sat cross-legged in front of the radio, receiving most of their information from the worried faces of their parents.

Lillian stood with one hand on the back of the couch to steady herself, the other pressed against her stomach. Like the others, she was stunned as she listened to the report about events that had already taken place over three hours ago: the United States had been attacked by Japan! Much of the U.S. fleet severely damaged.

Lillian followed Charles's eye to the morning newspaper folded next to the radio, the headlines seeming a mockery now: *Navy is Superior to Any Says Knox*. She wondered what Charles's thoughts were, what he was seeing in his mind. He had been in the Navy. She knew that he would feel the loss deeply, and understand the significance of the attack, in a way that she would not.

Annette and Lillian had tried to make the evening as normal as possible for the children, but the very air was different. Nothing looked or felt or tasted the same. Lillian's mind took off in a thousand different directions. Should she stay at Annette's with the children? Could she convince Charles to stay with her? Or would it be better to go home? Then the horrible thought that perhaps Charles would have to serve. She didn't want him out there in harm's way, bombs dropping, bullets flying; and yet they must all do whatever was required of them. She felt twisted by the two competing sentiments. Annette had remained rock solid throughout, helping to quell Lillian's disorderly fears.

Then the somber mood the following day as they once again gathered around the radio, listening to the President's speech: "a date which will live in infamy." The words "the Empire of Japan" had frightened Lillian, making her feel small, insignificant. Two mighty forces, empires, on either side of them. War was now coming from the Atlantic and the Pacific.

Later that evening, Annette had gotten out an old atlas, and she and Lillian searched for the location of the attack, and where the islands were in relation to the United States. They traced their fingers from the red nation of Japan, over the blue Pacific, to the sprinkle of pink islands called

Hawaii, a U.S. territory. It all seemed so far away, so unreal. But now there was talk that the Japanese empire might soon bomb San Francisco, Seattle, San Diego. And that the Germans would use the distraction to attack simultaneously from the East. They were trapped, like sitting ducks, unprepared, shocked, futilely flapping their wings in outrage.

Lillian had not wanted to leave Annette's. She wanted to stay up there where she thought they would be safer, until it was known what was really happening. Rumors and reports flooded the airwaves and newspapers about attacks off California, bombers spotted coming from Germany, submarines prowling both coasts. Lillian was afraid of returning to the city. She briefly considered leaving the boys with Annette, the way the people of London had sent their children to the north of England to be safe from The Blitz.

But neither Charles nor Lillian wanted to be separated from Tommy and Gabriel, or from each other. They had decided to go back, and face the war from home. They would have to return sooner or later. And they might not be able to get back if they waited too long – the trains might be restricted to military use.

Now, two days later, Lillian looked out the train window at the familiar landscape of her youth. The fallow fields, ribbed with snow; the houses with firewood stacked against them; the gardens with a few scraggly plants still staked. Everything looked so small and defenseless. She felt an overwhelming protectiveness for all these simple, ordinary things. The world had changed. The trucks that passed them, the gray sky, the glimpses of the Hudson – all were now imbued with another feeling. A darkness was coalescing, rising from the land, from the people. Fear. She saw it in the eyes of passengers who passed her, heard it in the worried tones from the seats behind them.

All leaves and furloughs were canceled, and the train was crowded with both military and civilian passengers. Several servicemen, most of them smoking, gathered in groups, and talked with an exaggerated show of bravado, threatening to show the Japs and Jerrys who was who.

Lillian gazed at the young men and thought, Will these slender boys be our saviors? These lads with the easy smiles and soft cheeks? She tried to envision them as they said their goodbyes. How could their mothers bear it? Tears started to her eyes, and she had the desire to do something for them – give them words of encouragement, or hand out apples and preserves, or press their hands in comfort. She wanted to treat them as she would her sons, with love and tenderness – but these soldiers had to be men now. Boyhood was forever behind them. Soon they would hold guns, grenades. Soon they would be shot at, injured, and perhaps killed. She imagined smoke, mud, barbed wire, water-filled trenches, hatred in an enemy eye. One young soldier sat gazing out the window, an unlit cigarette drooping from his fingers. Was he seeing his mother? Or his sweetheart? Or perhaps a vision of home, his family gathered around the dining table? Would he ever come back? Her eyes traveled from him, to Tommy, who was also staring out the window. Not many years separated them in age; in seven or eight years, it could be Tommy sitting there in uniform.

Many of the passengers gathered in groups and discussed the attack, speculating on what would happen next, where the Germans and Japs would strike. Gossip and fear combined with memories of the Great War. She heard the words *blackouts, enlistments, food shortages, treachery, espionage.*

Lillian raised her head and briefly scanned the passengers. As she looked up and down the aisle, she suddenly had the thought – what if there are spies among us, listening? She saw a man who appeared to be sleeping – what about him? Or her – an older woman who was clearly eaves-dropping on the couple behind her. Then Lillian noticed that a woman was looking directly at her with the same wary expression, sizing her up as perhaps a spy or traitor. The world had been turned upside down. Anger and hatred were already taking root. She saw it in the faces of other passengers, heard it in snippets of conversation. God help her, felt it in her own breast.

A heavy weariness began to overtake her. None of them had slept much the last two nights. She glanced over at Charles and the boys. Fatigue seemed to be affecting them all. Charles lay with his head back, his eyes closed. Gabriel had dozed off, the comic book still in his hands. Tommy sat in a daze, staring out at nothing – he would soon be asleep. Her darling boys. She would have to remember that they would be frightened, but might not know how to express it.

Lillian closed her eyes, and let herself be lulled by the gentle rocking of the train and the long sad pull of the train whistle, allowed these familiar things to lead her into the sweetness of sleep.

After what seemed like just a few minutes, she became aware of Charles speaking to the boys in low tones, of Gabriel asking Charles for the lunch hamper. She opened her eyes to see Charles lifting down the basket.

"Finally, you're awake!" said Tommy. "We're starving!"

"It's well past lunch," said Charles. "Thought we'd see what you and Annette packed for us."

Lillian sat up. "I must have dozed off." She looked out the window and rubbed her neck. She saw that Charles had draped his coat over her.

"You slept for almost two hours, Mom," said Tommy. "Look," he said, pointing out the window.

Lillian saw that the river had widened. She squeezed Charles's hand and smiled at Tommy and Gabriel. "I'm hungry too. We'll have a picnic lunch – along the Hudson!" She handed out sandwiches and apples, smiling at the boys' hearty appetite. When they were finished, Gabriel rummaged around in the hamper, and finding Annette's toffee, he passed it around.

Gabriel took a crunchy bite, and then held up the toffee in front of him. "Mommy, is this free?"

"Of course, it's free," she laughed. "Your Aunt Annette made it for us. Why?"

"Just wondering," answered Gabriel.

Tommy and Gabriel seemed to have forgotten that the country was at war. They sat with their faces close to the window, pointing out sights along the Hudson: tug boats and barges, a sail boat, two men fishing from the shore, a soaring bird of prey.

Lillian shifted her gaze to Charles. When something was bothering him, he tended to become quiet, and look away into the distance.

"What are you thinking about, Charles?"

He put on a cheerful face, obviously not wanting to burden her with whatever had been on his mind, she thought. Or perhaps he didn't want to worry the boys.

"Oh, just wondering how Mrs. Murphy is managing," he said. "I've never left her on her own before. Of course, Mason is there, but with three staff members enlisted, the office has been more of a challenge to manage. And now with war declared, I'll have to anticipate a further reduction in staff."

"Why don't you consider expanding the roles of the women, and hiring some? That's what's happening at the publishing house. Women are doing more reporting, more writing. I told you about Izzy – she's pretty much the floor manager now. She even got a raise. She's taking on more and more of Mr. Weeble's duties, now that he's been moved to Marketing and Advertising. Izzy loves it. She gets there early, leaves late."

Lillian briefly imagined her friend Izzy bustling around the office – seemingly happy, but with an ever-present anxiety underlying all her actions. Ever since Red joined the RAF; no, ever since he postponed their wedding. Izzy was not quite sure what his intentions were. And now he lay wounded somewhere in England.

In a flash, Lillian remembered Charles's earlier words to the boys about their next visit to Annette's: "maybe in the summer." She suddenly realized that it hadn't been a slip; he was too careful with his words to make such a mistake. Was he considering postponing *their* wedding?

She studied his face as she spoke, watching for any sign that might confirm her hunch. "Izzy loves her job, but I think she stays busy to keep from worrying about Red."

"How is he doing? Any word?"

"He's healing, though it seems to be taking a long time. Izzy worries about him constantly. She so regrets that they didn't marry before he left. That was their plan, you know. But seeing his buddy return home all shot up changed his mind."

Charles nodded, but remained quiet.

"Izzy thinks he's not telling her everything."

"Maybe he's trying to protect her," said Charles, looking away.

"Honesty is always best," Lillian said, somewhat defensively. Without stating it, the conversation had shifted to being about them. In her heart, she feared that he had already changed his mind.

They sat in silence for a few moments. Then Charles spoke decisively. "I think Red made the right decision, in postponing the wedding."

Lillian's stomach sank at his words. "No, he didn't. Not for Izzy. Not for them as a couple."

She waited for him to respond, but he just gazed out the window.

"Charles, you're not thinking of changing our plans." There was no reaction from him. "Are you?"

"No. But I think we're going to have to push the date back," he said. "Until we know what's up ahead."

"We never know what's up ahead."

Charles took a deep breath, and spoke quietly. "War has just been declared with Japan. War with

Germany is sure to follow. Let's wait and see how things develop."

Lillian sat back in her seat, upset at his words. She tried to envision their marriage taking place at some unknown date in the future. But she couldn't readjust her thoughts so quickly. It was too late to change their minds now. She already saw herself as his wife. He was already her husband. Countless times she had imagined greeting him as he walked in the door every night after work, sitting down together for dinner, waking up beside him, being with him some part of every day. And now that dream seemed to have crumbled into dust.

On Charles's lap lay the folded newspaper. In thick black letters Lillian saw the word *War*. She glanced out the window at the darkening day. The world was no longer her own.

# Chapter 3

∾

Lillian kept Tommy and Gabriel home from school the following day, ready to take cover if an air raid siren was sounded. She roused them early to get dressed, and then let them go back to bed with their clothes on. Next to the door, stood an emergency bag with food and extra clothing. She had stayed up late packing and repacking it, trying to decide what was most urgent. In the middle of the night, she had gotten up and added gloves to the bag. She remembered reading about the bombing of London and how everything was hot to the touch. Lillian now sat at the kitchen table with a cup of coffee, making a list of things to buy. She thought about Tommy and Gabriel's soft little hands, and added to her list: *First Aid Ointment. Gauze. Iodine.*

When they arrived at Grand Central the previous evening, they were surrounded by the chaos of scrambling crowds, everyone trying to get home as quickly as possible. Earlier in the day, there had been reports that a squadron of enemy planes was headed for Long Island, and the whole city was in a panic. Apparently the reports were based on a false tip that had turned into frightening rumors and quickly spread. Though no bombers had materialized, Lillian was still fearful of letting the boys out of her sight.

Her neighbor Mrs. Wilson had stopped by earlier to announce that her apartment building basement, three doors down from Lillian's brownstone, would be used as the main air raid shelter for their block. Mrs. Wilson had signed up as air raid warden, and was busy preparing and stocking the basement. Lillian was grateful for her efforts, not least because the boys' babysitter, Mrs. Kuntzman, lived in the same brownstone. There was some degree of comfort in knowing that, at least immediately before and after school, the boys would be as close as possible to the shelter. On the radio, she heard that schools would be kept open and locked down if there were more air raids. The thought of being separated from her boys, of not being there to help them, terrified her more than anything.

As the afternoon wore on, Tommy and Gabriel grew fussy and argumentative. A whole day of being cooped up was beginning to take its toll on them. It was now late afternoon, and Lillian was trying to coax one more drill out of them.

"Come on, boys," she said. "Just one more time, and then you can play."

Tommy groaned and stayed put on the couch. Gabriel walked over to the door and slumped against the wall.

They had already made three trips down to Mrs. Wilson's shelter. On the first two trips they brought an old blanket, an extra flashlight, a few canned vegetables, and some comic books. The last time was a dry run for a real air raid, and Lillian had made them run as quickly as possible. But the novelty had worn off, and the boys were now bored with the drill.

"One more for today," said Lillian. "Come on, Tommy. Ready?"

Tommy slid off the couch, rolled his eyes, and ambled to the door.

"Okay," said Lillian, waiting until she had Tommy's full attention. She took a deep breath and held it for a moment, looking from Tommy to Gabriel. "Go!" and they all ran down the stairs, out the door, down the sidewalk, and into the air raid shelter.

In the basement, an overhead light hung from the ceiling, illuminating the center of the open space. Mrs. Wilson was arranging some rolled bandages into a large first aid box. She spun around on hearing the boys running down the stairs, and clapped her hands.

"Bravo! Well done, Tommy! Very good, Gabriel! I'd say we're all set."

"Nobody else had to stay home," grumbled Tommy.

"Yeah, Billy went to school," added Gabriel.

"It's hard to know what to do," Lillian said to Mrs. Wilson. "I thought it best to keep them home."

Mrs. Wilson closed the lid of the first aid box. "Well, all we can do is be prepared. I suppose the children will be just as safe at school as in their homes. Perhaps even safer," she added as an afterthought.

Lillian nodded, understanding that a bombed school would be responded to as quickly as possible.

"After all," continued Mrs. Wilson, "this will likely go on for quite some time. Mark my words." She took Lillian's arm and whispered, "I think it's best to let them go to school tomorrow. Keep things as normal as possible for them."

"I suppose so," sighed Lillian. "I'll let Mrs. Kuntzman know that we've returned early." Lillian started to go up the basement steps, and then turned around. "I'm glad you're taking charge with this, Mrs. Wilson. It makes me feel safer."

"Well," said Mrs. Wilson, putting her fists on her hips and looking around at what she had accomplished in a mere twenty-four hours, "I do like getting things done. Go on ahead. I'll be right up. I need to have a word with Mrs. Kuntzman, myself."

On hearing the voices of the neighborhood children returning from school, Tommy and Gabriel had dashed up the basement stairs, and were now gathered around them, listening to what they missed out on at school.

"Tommy," Lillian called out to him. "You and Gabriel stay here while I call on Mrs. Kuntzman, okay? You'll stay put?"

Tommy turned to her and mouthed silently, "Yes!"

She knew that expression; Tommy was embarrassed in front of his friends. She could hear his argument: first he had to stay home from school, and now she was treating him like a baby.

Lillian left the boys with their friends, and walked up the brownstone steps to Mrs. Kuntzman's.

The elderly babysitter answered the knock at her door wearing a bright green calico apron with a trace of flour on both her apron and her cheek.

"Hello, Mrs. Hapsey! Ach, you returned early from your journey?"

"We thought it best to come back while we could. If it's all right, I'll drop the boys off tomorrow and Friday."

"Yes, of course! Only a few days and already I miss Tommy and Gabriel," she laughed. "Oh, dear," she said, suddenly remembering. "On Friday my daughter will come to take me shopping, so in afternoon I won't be here for the boys."

"That's all right. I'll arrange to take a half-day. Unless you'd rather have the whole day. I could switch with one of the girls –"

"No, no. I look forward to my breakfasts with Tommy and Gabriel. Friday morning is fine."

Just then, Mrs. Wilson opened the vestibule door, and Lillian was surprised when Mrs. Kuntzman made a quick duck into her apartment.

"There's no escaping *me*, Mrs. Kuntzman," called out Mrs. Wilson. She then addressed Lillian. "Now, Mrs. Hapsey, perhaps *you* can talk some sense into Mrs. Kuntzman. I've told her repeatedly that *if* there is another air raid siren, she *must* come down to the basement with the rest of us."

Mrs. Kuntzman stepped back out into the hall, and smiled sweetly, but spoke firmly. "And I say, if Tommy and Gabriel are here with me, then I come down."

"But you *must* come down, in any case," insisted Mrs. Wilson. "As air raid warden, it's my responsibility to make sure that you do."

Mrs. Kuntzman batted down the idea with her hand. "No one want me there with my German accent. I come down with Tommy and Gabriel. Is final." She folded her flour-dusted hands in front of her, and again smiled sweetly.

Both women looked to Lillian as the arbitrator who would surely take their side.

"Well," said Lillian, facing Mrs. Kuntzman, "I'm sure everyone will want you to be safe with them –"

"Ha!" said Mrs. Kuntzman. "You don't know that man on third floor."

"You leave Mr. Redmond to me," said Mrs. Wilson. "If he has *his* way, he won't have me there either."

"I live on first floor," continued Mrs. Kuntzman. "Close enough to basement."

Again both women looked to Lillian. She turned from one woman to the other, not wanting to offend either. "I'm sure Mrs. Kuntzman can make up her own mind about what is right for her." Mrs. Wilson's raised eyebrows spurred Lillian to balance her advice. "Though I do hope you'll take every precaution," she said to Mrs. Kuntzman.

Mrs. Kuntzman gave a brisk single nod. "End of matter."

Mrs. Wilson threw her hands up. "Well! You may have won this skirmish, Mrs. Kuntzman, but I intend to make sure that *all* tenants come to the air raid shelter at the first sound of the sirens."

Mrs. Kuntzman made a little hm-hmm sound that Lillian took to mean, *we'll see about that!*

"Well," said Mrs. Wilson, taking off her checked headscarf and stuffing it into her coat pocket, "I must go and tend to the mess upstairs." She waved her hand in the air above her. "Harry turned the place upside down searching for his bird-watching binoculars. He's signed up to be a spotter. Up on the roof." She began her march up the stairs to the fourth floor. "Good day, ladies." She leaned over the railing and fixed an eye on Mrs. Kuntzman. "To be continued."

"Good bye, Mrs. Wilson," said Lillian.

Mrs. Kuntzman leaned into Lillian and whispered, "Bossy woman. Make a good general."

Lillian laughed at her assessment of Mrs. Wilson. "She just wants to make sure that you're safe. I won't keep you, Mrs. Kuntzman. I just wanted to let you know that we're back."

"Tell Tommy and Gabriel I make waffles for them tomorrow."

"They'll be delighted. We brought apples for you from my sister's orchard. And some cherry preserves."

"Ach, good! I make cherry krapfen for Tommy and Gabriel. Those boys love donuts best of all." Mrs. Kuntzman put a hand on Lillian's arm.

"Mrs. Hapsey, don't worry about Tommy and Gabriel. I make sure they go inside school, then I come back home. If there is air raid siren here, I take them to basement. Make Mrs. Wilson happy."

Lillian said goodbye, suppressing a laugh as Mrs. Kuntzman cast a quick glance up the stairs before closing her door.

Returning to her brownstone, Lillian saw her next door neighbor, Mrs. Kinney, talking to a few of the other women on the street. Over the past year, Tommy and Gabriel had become good friends with the Kinney boys closest to their ages, Mickey and Billy. Tommy and Mickey played on the same baseball team, and sometimes worked on their homework together. Billy was a year older than Gabriel and was starting to spend more time with the older boys, sometimes leaving Gabriel with no one to play with.

Lillian saw that several groups of people were gathered up and down the street. She had noticed that ever since the attack on Sunday, people tended to band together. She had observed it up at Annette's when they went into town the day after the attack; everyone stood in clusters. And again on the train, where everyone gathered into groups, sitting on the seat arms or bent over the seat backs. Perhaps they were all trading information; or maybe no one wanted to be alone. She had the same urge herself, to be around people, to hear what they had to say.

Lillian joined Mrs. Kinney and the other women and listened in on their discussion about yesterday's air raid sirens and the best course of action concerning the children going to school.

After a few moments, Tommy and Gabriel ran up with Mickey and Billy.

"See, Mom," said Tommy. "I told you! We should have gone to school. Everyone got a handbook on air raids but me!"

"Yeah, Mommy!" added Gabriel, tugging on her sleeve. "I missed the air raid drill at school. Billy said everyone got a tag with their name and address on it and got to go on a walk outside."

Mrs. Kinney shrugged at Lillian. "Like you, I didn't want to send my boys to school, but their father thought it was best. He walked them there, and I picked them up. I was sick with worry all day. It's difficult to know what to do."

"Keep cool," said one of the women. "Those were Mayor La Guardia's exact words. And Mrs. Wilson said we should stick to our routines, especially where the children are concerned."

"That's hard to do with sirens going off," said Mrs. Kinney. "But I suppose she's right."

Lillian put an arm around her boys. "Come on. Let's go home. You can go to school tomorrow."

"Yippee!" said Gabriel.

"Mom," asked Mickey, "can Tommy and Gabe come up? I want to show them my new baseball cards."

"Is that all right with you, Mrs. Hapsey?" asked Mrs. Kinney.

"If you're sure they won't be in your way," said Lillian.

"Not at all," laughed Mrs. Kinney. "This way I can start dinner without them getting in my hair."

The boys were already clamoring up the stairs. "I want you home before dark!" Lillian called out after them.

Lillian went back to her apartment and placed the macaroni casserole she made earlier into the oven to bake. She tidied the boys' bedroom and set out their school clothes, and then went to her room and opened her closet, deciding on what she would wear to the office the next day. She was glad to be returning to work, and yet the idea of sitting at the switchboard filled her with a sense of defeat. The monotony of her position was starting to wear on her. She was grateful to have a job, yet she couldn't help but feel that she was wasting her time. Especially with the country now at war. It seemed that she should be doing something besides answering calls all day for a publishing house.

The familiar knock at her door was a welcome distraction. She thought Charles might have to work late and wasn't sure if she would see him. When she opened the door, she saw that he held a bag of groceries and a newspaper.

"I brought you a few things from Mancetti's." He bent to kiss her lightly on the cheek. "The boys?" he asked, looking around.

"Over at the Kinney's. Can you stay for dinner?"

He shook his head. "I had a late lunch, and I have a mound of papers to catch up on." He set the bag of groceries on the kitchen table.

Lillian reached inside the bag and took out a can of coffee and several canned goods. "Sugar?" she asked, seeing two bags at the bottom.

Charles hung his coat and hat on the hall tree. "And canned milk. They say there won't be food shortages, but I thought it wouldn't hurt to take Annette's advice. Especially with your holiday baking coming up."

"You and my sister. Always watching out for me."

"And Mrs. Mancetti. She knew we were away and set aside the sugar and coffee for you. People are already hoarding." Charles shook his head lightly. "The tension was pretty thick in there."

Lillian stacked the canned goods in the cupboard. "Because of the hoarding?"

"Because the Mancetti's are Italian. And we're sure to be at war with Italy soon."

"Oh, my God." Lillian leaned against the counter. "I didn't even think of that. I'll stop by tomorrow and thank her."

"When I arrived, Mrs. Mancetti was putting out a bag of food for some poor wretch, hiding it under the bench, where her husband wouldn't see, no doubt." Charles took the newspaper and sat on the couch.

"She often helps people," Lillian said, pouring them each a glass of wine. "The Mancetti's are a part of our neighborhood. I hope people won't treat them any differently."

"War will change the way people think," said Charles. "You can count on that."

Lillian handed him his glass of wine, and sat down next to him. She thought he seemed tired and wondered if she appeared the same way. There was no denying the strain of the past few days.

Charles took a sip, leaned back, and gave a deep sigh. "You never know how people are going to react. Mrs. Murphy, for example. I've never seen her so subdued. I didn't expect that kind of reaction from her – I thought she would be feistier if anything, full of advice and opinions. She barely said two words today. Not like her at all."

"That is strange," said Lillian. She had talked with Mrs. Murphy several times and had a hard time imagining her subdued. She was one of the most energetic and cheerful people Lillian had ever met. But then she had noticed subtle changes even in her own behavior: less patience with the boys, more frustration with little things.

Charles held the newspaper for Lillian to see the headlines: *Roosevelt Sees a Long, World-Wide War*.

"Dear God," she exclaimed, taking the paper. "A world-wide war! I just can't take it all in." She scanned the front page, and then set it aside on the coffee table, as if pushing the news away from her. "I heard on the radio that they won't be reporting the weather anymore; they're afraid the enemy will use the information against us. And they say it's even worse on the West Coast. Blackouts, curfews. Everyone is so afraid." Lillian looked up at Charles. "Do you think they'll bomb us?"

"It's hard to say. At least we're on the defensive now. They won't catch us off guard a second time." He gazed into the empty fireplace, his thoughts far away.

Lillian wondered if he was thinking about his sister. He had tried, unsuccessfully, to call her from upstate. "Were you able to get through to Kate?"

"No. And they've asked people not to tie up the lines with unessential phone calls."

"Are you worried about her and her family?"

He raised his eyebrows as if considering the situation. "I'm glad they're in Illinois. It seems farther away from any threat. Though her sons will be called to duty soon." He thought about this a moment, and took another sip of wine. "I suppose one of them will be able to stay and help out."

"They'll have to. Kate and the girls can't run the farm all on their own. The girls are barely what – fourteen or so?"

"Thirteen and fifteen," said Charles. "Thank God we went there over the summer. Travel will surely be restricted soon. It could be years before we get back there again."

Lillian watched as Charles rubbed his face, and then rested his arms on his knees. The Midwest now seemed very far away.

Charles's sister was almost fifty now, and on her own since her husband died five years ago. But from what Lillian had seen of her, Kate was an extremely capable woman. Still, Lillian knew that Charles was concerned about her. He felt terrible that he had lost touch with her for so long – over twenty-five years. Their reunion over the summer had been bittersweet, stirring up painful memories. But the bond between the two had been unmistakable. Reconnecting with his sister after so many years had filled Charles with a new happiness; suddenly he had family again, nieces and nephews, another person who shared his history, a sense of being rooted.

Lillian remembered the walks and conversations she had with Kate. It had been a pleasure getting to know her and her family. Kate's four sons, all in their teens and early twenties, had treated Tommy and Gabriel just like little brothers, taking them around the farm on the tractor, driving them into town for ice cream, playing games and rough-housing with them.

And Lillian had met Rachel, Charles's childhood sweetheart, whose farm was not too far from Kate's. Lillian had often thought of her since then, especially lately.

"Would you have married Rachel?" she asked, thinking out loud.

Charles jerked his head up and frowned. "What made you ask that?"

"I don't know. I guess I was just thinking about our visit there."

Charles sighed and leaned his head back on the couch. "I don't know, Lillian. That seems irrelevant now."

They sat quietly for a few minutes, each in their own thoughts.

"Charles, I've been thinking. And I really think we should stick to our plans. To get married in May. I keep thinking about Izzy. Red joked that if he came back in one piece they would marry on the day he returned. And now he's been lying wounded for months. His letters have tapered off. Izzy is miserable."

Charles waited a moment, and then shook his head. "Everything is so volatile and unsure. I think it's better for us to wait."

"But Charles, we've already decided. We already told Annette and Bernie. And Kate. They're all so happy for us."

Charles avoided Lillian's questioning eyes, and let his gaze fall somewhere out in front of him. "I wrote to Kate yesterday. To tell her we were fine. And that we were considering postponing the wedding."

Lillian set her glass down and felt her temper rise. "*We* didn't consider anything. You have. Without any input from me."

"It's not like that." He gently put a hand on her shoulder. "There's just too much uncertainty right now. I will most likely be called to serve. It could be in the Atlantic, or Pacific. There's no knowing what's up ahead. What could happen."

Lillian had already thought of that possibility, but it made her want to marry Charles sooner rather than later, and she had expected him to feel the same way. The threat of being separated now dangled constantly in front of her.

"That may be," she said. "But it has nothing to do with us getting married."

Charles simply looked away. "It's best to wait."

When he left, Lillian felt that something had come between them. She tried to tell herself that disagreements were to be expected. It would be a part of their lives together. She couldn't put her finger on it, but he seemed different ever since they came back home from their trip upstate. More distant. He seemed to have taken a step back. Lillian assumed that it was because of the war, but perhaps there was another reason. Perhaps he was having second thoughts about marriage, and the war gave him an excuse to back out of it.

\*

After dinner, Lillian cleaned up the kitchen, half of her mind on Charles, the other half on Tommy and Gabriel. The boys were supposed to take their baths after dinner, and Gabriel had finished with his. But when Lillian listened for sounds of Tommy getting ready, she didn't hear anything. She went to their room and saw Tommy stretched out on his bed reading.

Gabriel sat next to Tommy, looking over his shoulder at the *Captain America* comic book he was reading. "Read it out loud, Tommy. Please?" he asked. A drop of water fell from his wet hair and landed on the page.

Tommy pulled the comic book away from Gabriel. "Go get your own book! I don't want you breathing down my neck!" He sat up, and scooted to the other end of the bed.

"Come on, boys, no arguing," said Lillian, suddenly feeling very tired. "Tommy, you were supposed to take your bath."

Lillian took the towel that Gabriel had tossed on his bed and began rubbing his hair dry.

"It wouldn't hurt you to pay a little more attention to your brother, Tommy."

"I'm just getting to the good part, and reading to Gabriel gets in the way. He asks too many questions."

"No, I don't," said Gabriel.

"I'll read to you after my bath, Gabriel" said Lillian. "Look at one of your picture books until then." She took a comb from their dresser and began combing his wet hair.

"Mommy," said Gabriel. "What will we call Mr. Drooms? Dad?"

Tommy gave a little snort of amusement. "Dad," he said, trying out the word. He sat up, as if in imaginary greeting: "Hi, Dad! How was work, Dad?"

Tommy and Gabriel let out a peal of laughter.

"Hiya, Papa!" Gabriel tried out, causing them to laugh all the more.

"For the time being, he is Mr. Drooms. We might have to wait a little longer now before getting married." She felt both boys look up at her, waiting for an explanation. "Because of the war."

"What difference does that make?" asked Tommy. "Everything else still goes on. Can I stop doing chores until after the war?"

"Go take your bath, Tommy. I want you both in bed in ten minutes. It's a school night."

Lillian made sure Tommy started his bath-water, and then she went to her room and slipped into her robe. She hoped that a hot bath would take away some of the tension she had felt all day. She pinned up her hair, and then stopped to listen. She heard Tommy splashing away in the bathtub, but she thought she heard Gabriel talking in his room.

She went to check up on him, and saw that he had emptied the bag of twigs he had collected up at Annette's. He was now sorting them into piles.

"Gabriel, what are you doing? You're going to get your hands all dirty again."

"I'm putting the sticks into big and little sizes."

She stepped inside and looked at Gabriel, then at the piles. "Well, you're doing a good job. Who were you talking to?"

"Tiny."

A small smile escaped Lillian. "Your new friend?"

Gabriel nodded. "The sticks are for him."

Lillian sat on Gabriel's bed and watched him sort a few more sticks. Perhaps the news of war upset him in ways she hadn't thought of. Maybe having an imaginary friend made him feel secure in the midst of so much uncertainty.

"I had a friend like that when I was about your age." Lillian gazed at the ceiling, remembering. "Annabelle was her name. I haven't thought of her in years. She could fly. She was a beautiful fairy, with blue dragonfly wings. She would fly out before me and tell me what was up ahead, so I always knew what to expect."

She waited for Gabriel to say something, but he just looked up and smiled.

"Can Tiny fly?" she asked.

"No, Mom. He just walks."

Lillian bit her lip. "Is he a little boy?"

Gabriel sat back on his heels, considering how to answer. "He's kind of an in-between person."

Lillian gazed at Gabriel, thinking that he had always been an imaginative child. "Do you talk to him often?"

"Just when I have something to tell him."

She didn't want to disturb his illusion, but she wanted to make sure that everything was all right with him. "What were you talking to him about – just now?"

"I was telling him about the sticks."

"And does he talk back to you?"

"Kind of. He said that's how he used to talk to his mom. After she left. He talked to her in his head, and he said she always answered him back. So that's how we talk, too."

Lillian leaned forward and hugged Gabriel. "I'm not going anywhere, sweetheart. You know that, don't you? I'm going to stay right here with you. Even after I get married."

Gabriel smiled up at her again. He tidied the smallest bundle, and wrapped some string around it. "There. He's going to give them to his brother."

"Tiny has a brother? Well, that's nice for him." She heard the bath water draining and stood up. "I bet he reads to Tiny, doesn't he?"

"He used to," said Gabriel.

Lillian wondered if Tommy's pushing Gabriel aside made him sadder than she had realized. Did an imaginary friend fill in the gap?

Tommy soon jumped into bed, taking his comic book with him.

Lillian kissed Gabriel on the head. "Finish up. I'll come in and read to you after my bath."

"Okay, Mommy."

Lillian brushed back Tommy's wet hair and put a hand on his cheek.

"I can read by myself, Mom," said Tommy.

"All right," she said, giving his nose a tweak.

Lillian left the room, wondering why she had never given Annabelle a sister. She smiled, thinking that she probably had wanted her all to herself. Much as she wanted Charles.

She turned on the water, reached for the slender indigo bottle with its intricate silver stopper, and poured out a few drops of lavender oil into the water. So much had changed in just a few days. Her small rituals, and the history that imbued them, seemed even more important now; she would need them to help keep her grounded in the coming months.

As she sank into the hot, fragrant water, she gave a deep sigh of pleasure. One by one, the worries and tension that had been clenched inside her released and dissolved away. Her shoulders unknotted, her arms and legs lightened.

The perfume of the bath oil stirred up memories of dusky flower gardens and lavender-scented sheets. She had made the lavender oil with Kate and her daughters over the summer. They had gathered bunches and bunches of the purple flowers in the early morning, before the bumblebees were active, and dried them in the heat of the day. Then in the evenings, they gathered around the large, wooden kitchen table, talking and laughing, and making lavender oil and sachets. They let the flowers steep in jars of oil for a few days before straining and adding fresh flowers, repeating this until the scent became strong. And they took tiny bits of silk and sewed small sachets of lavender to tuck inside drawers and linen cupboards. By the end of the trip, Lillian had a bottle of lavender oil to take home with her, along with several sachets. About a week after their return to New York, Charles had surprised her one day with the beautiful indigo bottle to store the oil in. It was one of her prized possessions, reminding her of the gentle summer.

Lillian let her mind wander back to the two weeks they had spent on Kate's farm in Illinois. It was the first time she and Charles had taken a trip together, and it had helped to seal their relationship.

The trip had been wonderful in so many ways. Tommy and Gabriel were thrilled to be in the country, running through the corn fields, jumping from the hay loft. And she loved the tranquility of the farm, the crickets at night, the breathtaking sunsets over the fields, and the rhythms of the day that were so closely connected to the land.

After just a few days, Lillian found herself developing her own routines. Every evening, just after the sun dipped into the cornfield, and every morning, when the world was still soft with dew, she strolled around the farmhouse yard, admiring the flowers that grew in abundance. Kate identified many of them as old plantings that had been there since the farm was first established: spirea, wild roses, hydrangeas, and climbing jasmine that nearly covered one side of the house and chimney, scenting the whole yard with lush sweetness in the afternoon heat. To these Kate had added flowers that would grow on their own, with little need of tending: daylilies, white and yellow daisies, holly-hock of all colors reaching up alongside the barn, and near the herb garden, mounds of lavender. These flowers were planted in good black soil, with no promise other than sunshine and water – and they had thrived on the freedom of being left on their own.

Kate often joined Lillian in her early morning walks, and together they clipped flowers to make simple bouquets for the kitchen table and for Lillian's bedroom.

These simple pleasures reminded Lillian of her girlhood in upstate New York, where she, too, lived close to the land, the abundance and beauty of nature a part of her daily life. In some ways, the trip had made her homesick – she missed the pleasure of female company that she used to have with her sister and mother, the small details they wove into the day that made it richer: something as simple as arranging flowers in a glass jar, preparing a special dessert, or just sitting on the porch and talking. Being with Kate and her daughters was like going back in time, and Lillian had loved it.

But she most loved the trip because of how good it had been for Charles. He and Kate had a chance to catch up on all the years he had stayed away, and Kate's children adored him. They had always heard about their uncle, and hung on his every word. The boys wanted to hear about his years in the Navy; the girls wanted to hear all about New York City.

Lillian wondered why she was thinking so much about the trip lately. For some reason, a persistent image kept surfacing in her mind, unbidden, stubborn – ever since Charles had suggested postponing their wedding. She wasn't sure why she was linking the two.

The image was sharp, fresh – as if it had just happened; or perhaps it was the replaying of it again and again in her mind that kept it so. It was on one of their last days there, the afternoon when they were visited by Charles's childhood sweetheart, Rachel. Her husband and sons were away at the State Fair, so it was just Rachel and her daughter who had driven over and stayed the day.

In the afternoon, Kate's two daughters and Rachel's daughter decided to gather hickory nuts. There was a pasture full of the tall trees down the country road, not far from the farm. Lillian and Kate were busy hanging laundry on the clothesline, but the girls had convinced Charles and Rachel to join them. The girls were in their early teens, and frolicked with all the energy and light-heartedness of youth, alternately whispering, and then bursting into laughter.

Lillian helped Kate finish the laundry, and then sat with her on the front porch, shucking corn for dinner. A beautiful August day surrounded them in all its fullness and simple charm. A gentle breeze rustled the leaves high in the pin oaks, and fluttered the laundry on the clothes line, causing the white billowing sheets to snap softly now and then. The wide porch surrounded them with views of the corn and soybean fields stretching to the horizon. To the east stood a cluster of tall trees, their leaves a dark, dusty, late-summer green, with some leaves already edged in brown. And before them, Kate's flowers along the lane – a tall tangle of orange, yellow, white, and blues – tiger lilies and daisies, cornflowers and asters.

Lillian lifted her face to catch the afternoon breeze, and caught the scent of honeysuckle that covered the fence along the lane. The wind alternately muffled and then sharpened the sounds of Tommy and Gabriel playing horseshoes with Kate's sons: dull thuds as the horseshoes fell on the earth, clinks of metal as they hit their mark or landed on each other, mixed with clapping, laughing, good-natured disputing. Lillian had felt suffused with a sense of well-being, surrounded by an earthy loveliness.

She had an ear of corn in her hand, and with a few quick downward pulls, the stiff, rough husk skirted the juicy cob. She snapped off the husk and tossed it into the pail at her feet, and then pulled off the brown tassel. Then she stopped a moment as she pulled away the delicate corn silk, admiring the pale gold color, and thinking – in each ear of corn this silky beauty, something so fine and delicate that just gets tossed away. And yet it must serve some purpose, she mused. She let her eyes sweep the wide cornfields that lay to the west of the farm; the dry brown stalks shuddered lightly in the breeze, their rough husks full of the silky beauty inside. She looked down at the pale green-gold, gliding it between her fingers.

Kate straightened and put her hands to her lower back. "There they are now."

Lillian lifted her head and saw the girls coming down the dirt road, their summer dresses and long hair flying, as they ran ahead of Charles and Rachel.

Kate gave a sudden look at Lillian. "You're very like Rachel, now that I think of it."

Lillian shaded her eyes, watching them as they neared the farm. From the dirt road, the girls took a short cut and squeezed between a break in the fence, laughing as they got tangled up in the old weeping willow branches that swayed in the breeze.

Charles stepped ahead of Rachel and held the branches aside for her to pass, almost like parting a curtain. They walked up the lane, Charles with his hands clasped behind, strolling with an ease Lillian had never seen in him before. Something about that image of him walking with his old sweetheart, and the delicacy of the corn silk between her fingers, had stayed with her. Buried tenderness, memories of youth. It had both moved and pained her.

It wasn't jealousy that she felt. She had sincerely liked Rachel, and had so enjoyed that evening with her and Kate's family. Rachel was a lovely woman, with a deep rich laugh, and a quick smile. Still beautiful. Charles had seemed protective of her.

When Lillian had later asked him about their outing, and what he and Rachel had talked about, he had shrugged and dismissed it.

"Nothing, really. Mostly about now. The threat of war, her brother Caleb and his family." A shadow of sorrow crossed his face only once. "And I apologized. For my behavior back then. I hurt her — and everyone. She loved the twins, too. She was there at the accident. It must have been so difficult for her, but at the time I couldn't see anyone's pain but my own. It was selfish of me. But she had only kind, gentle words for me. No blame."

Lillian knew that Charles had needed to hear those words, and she was appreciative of Rachel's tenderness. The entire visit had helped Charles to heal from the haunting memories. A kind of transformation had taken place in him, and it seemed that he had finally made peace with his past. She knew that he had always blamed himself for having dallied with Rachel while his little brother and sister were falling through the ice. Lillian was grateful that his time with Rachel had served as balm to his old wound.

But Lillian also had to admit to another feeling. She had the impression that the old love, that budding young love between two twelve-year-olds, had lain dormant under the cold earth these long years, buried, along with the twins – and had now, years later, blossomed. The petals could finally unfurl and drink in the sun's warmth, not in this world, but in that past, in that world of his youth.

At the time, Lillian had felt that it had somehow come between her and Charles. And yet, she thought, didn't she have that same sweetness of memory with her first love, with Tom, and their early years of courting? Like a bit of corn silk inside of us – the tender sweetness of youth, first love, the promise of days ahead – a silky beauty that pads our youth and protects the early dreams, so that they may develop into fruitfulness.

She wouldn't want Charles to be without anything that helped him. And for that reason, she had a sort of love for Rachel. Along with the unreasonable regret that she herself was not the source of all sweetness and balm in his life.

# Chapter 4

For two days and two nights, Mrs. Murphy went over and over her behavior in the department store, thoroughly ashamed of herself. After fretting all day, she decided that she must make amends that very night. The encounter with Brendan Sullivan had been so completely unexpected, that she had lost her nerve, and simply ran away from him rather than confront the past she had so definitively shelved away. It was so long ago that she had moved from Boston to New York. Full forty years had passed since then. She had found a career, and had eventually made a life for herself. Drooms Accounting had been the core of her world for over twenty years now. And she was happy.

She had been living her life in the clear, crystal water of her own making. She knew what was what, and where her life was going, exactly what to expect. Seeing Brendan had been a convulsive stirring up of all the old sediment, clouding everything up again. She felt confused, sad, and ashamed of her behavior. It was not the behavior of the woman she thought she had become. She would go back to the department store and apologize. At least that way she could look herself in the eye again.

After leaving work, she went to the ladies' room and stood before the mirror to check her appearance. She tidied her hair and powdered her nose. Yes, she thought, scanning her reflection, all in all, she was happy. She snapped her compact closed, returned it to her purse, and then put on her hat and gloves, and looked again. Well, content, anyway. Satisfied. Her posture sank ever so slightly. Wasn't she? She thought she had been. But seeing Brendan had pulled back the cover of an old empty drawer inside herself.

What must he think of me? Running away like that. She squared her shoulders again and lifted her chin. You were a coward once, but you were young then. You're a grown woman now, and you'll face up to things as you have ever since. She gave her reflection a quick nod, as if all had been settled.

She left the building, and boarded the bus back down to the department store. Her only thought as she stared out the window, was that the poor man at least deserved the common courtesy she showed to everyone else. He's just an old friend, she told herself.

She got off the bus, crossed the avenue, and stood in front of the department store. Just an old friend. She rode the escalator up to the North Pole and hung back awhile, not wanting to interfere with his work a second time. When there was a lull in the line, she stepped forward and faced him. She put on a practiced smile and waited for Santa to turn. But when he did, her smile dropped to the floor and shattered. It was a different man. Not Brendan.

It was some other Santa altogether, with a ridiculous looking beard and moustache. No child would be fooled by that, she thought indignantly as she walked up to the sales clerk.

"Excuse me, sir. I was here the other night, and there was a different Santa."

"We have four or five of them," replied the frazzled clerk, taking a train set from a customer to ring up.

"Well, there was one with a real beard – so authentic. I wanted to bring my nephew in to see him. Might you know when –"

"Sorry, ma'am. They rotate their schedules. I can't keep track of them all. Why don't you check back tomorrow?"

Mrs. Murphy nodded and stepped back. She had worked herself up to seeing Brendan again, had rehearsed her lines over and over. Was prepared. Would she come back night after night and try to find him? What if he didn't return?

She tried to ignore her disappointment and walked through several departments, thinking that perhaps he would be somewhere else in the store. She walked through the men's department, and inspected a few shirts, and glanced over the ties, before moving on. Then she went to the housewares department, feeling silly as she pretended to be interested in a set of canisters. Then down to the first floor, where she absent-mindedly unfolded and then folded a few scarves on display. She kept replaying the way she had fled from the store, and worried what Brendan must think of her, how he must feel.

Her attention was caught by an arrangement of Christmas snow globes on the counter, each with a little world of its own inside: children building a snowman, St. Nicholas carrying a bag of toys, a snowy village, a Christmas tree. She didn't want to leave. She wanted to try to put things right, and was terribly disappointed that Brendan wasn't there. She picked up the snow globe with the Christmas tree inside, and shook it, telling herself that she would leave when the last tiny flakes sifted to the bottom. She set it on the counter and watched the snowy world inside calm and settle itself. Then she took a deep breath, and turned to leave the store. It was no use. Brendan clearly wasn't there.

She walked through the crowded first floor, surprised at the heavy feeling of regret inside her. Was it because she was denied the chance to redeem herself? Or was it because she had looked forward to seeing Brendan again?

The merry shoppers streamed around her as she made her way out of the store. She was almost to the front door when she felt a light touch on her arm. She turned.

And there he was. A surge of joy shot through her and turned her cheeks pink; she hoped he wouldn't notice.

"I was hoping you might come back," Brendan said. "I flatter myself you've been looking for me." He spoke in a light playful tone, but a sad hopefulness hung about his eyes.

Mrs. Murphy thought she had been prepared. But now that Brendan was before her, she found herself stumbling around the truth again.

"Oh, goodness me, I was just doing a little holiday shopping. Though I *am* glad to see you again. I wanted to apologize for the other night. I intended to wait, but I suddenly remembered –" Impossible. Nothing but the truth would answer to his gentle, trusting eyes.

"I'm sorry, Brendan. I'm afraid I have no excuse for my behavior."

"No matter. I didn't mean to surprise you so. Or upset you."

They stepped aside to make room for the passing shoppers laden with bags. A few children lifted their curious faces to Brendan. Though he was dressed in a blue and gray tweed coat and cap, his resemblance to Santa Claus was unmistakable.

Mrs. Murphy laughed at the children's curiosity. "Even out of your costume, you still look like Santa."

He gave a light tug at his beard. "It's this. To be trimmed after the holiday. Where are you off to now? Could I prevail on you to have a cup of tea with me? Just for old time's sake."

"The truth is Brendan, that's the only reason I came. I was hoping you would be here. I would love to have tea with you."

He became all smiles and twinkly blue eyes again. "That'd be grand! Come. There's a little place just around the corner."

Just as they were about to leave, Mr. Mason from the accounting firm walked in through the revolving doors, and nearly bumped into them.

"Well, hello Mrs. Murphy! Doing some shopping?"

Mrs. Murphy blushed a deeper pink. "Good evening, Mr. Mason. Yes, a little Christmas shopping for the nieces and nephews. And you?"

"My wife has a few things on layaway." He sensed her discomfort and decided to move on. "Well, I'll see you tomorrow then," he said, tipping his hat to them, and then pushing on through the crowd.

Brendan slapped his thigh. "Mrs. Murphy, is it? So you married a man with the same name as yours? Now, what are the odds of that?" he laughed, and held the door open for her.

They walked to the little café, briefly discussing the news of the war and where they were when they heard about the attack on Pearl Harbor. Once inside the café, they found a table near the window. Mrs. Murphy folded her hands in front of her and glanced outside while Brendan hung up their coats. The city glittered with lights from the traffic, the shop windows, the street lamps, and a flow of sounds filled the air – brakes and horns, the merry clanging from a Salvation Army bell ringer, the "Extra, Extra" of the newsboys selling the evening papers. Shoppers and workers crowded the sidewalks, all rushing home to someone.

For a moment, Mrs. Murphy felt that she was part of all that wonderful whirlwind; she felt young and hopeful, as if something wonderful were about to happen. She had forgotten that such a feeling existed, and tried to push it back down.

"Shall we share a pot of tea, then?" asked Brendan, sitting down, and gesturing to the waiter.

"That would be lovely!" she said. Even the act of ordering a pot of tea seemed momentous, something to be taken note of and stored away for future delight.

They glanced at the menu and ordered sandwiches. Mrs. Murphy smiled up at the delightfully kind waiter who brought the tea. What's wrong with me? she couldn't help but wonder. This is just a casual meal with an old friend. This is just a pot of tea. No need to make more out of it than it is.

She sat up straight, snatching glances at Brendan, trying to see what the years had done to him. He looked well. Happy. Just as she had always imagined him.

"So, Mrs. Murphy!" Brendan said playfully. He cleared the space in front of him and leaned his elbows on the table, bringing him another inch or two closer to her. "What have you been doing these last forty years? Have you been living here in New York City all this time?"

"Yes. Nearly forty years. I originally moved here to help my sister Maureen with her growing brood."

"Your second eldest sister, if memory serves me," said Brendan.

"That's right." Mrs. Murphy lifted the teapot and poured them each a cup. "She had two children at the time, and another on the way."

"Kathleen was the eldest in your family," Brendan said, setting the sugar bowl in front of her. "Followed by Gavin. Then James. Jamesy, as you called him."

Mrs. Murphy smiled, and stirred some sugar into her tea, wondering if Brendan meant anything by his display of memory. She hoped he wouldn't start asking questions about the past. Surely he would have the good grace to keep the conversation on the present.

"I see you still take two spoons of sugar in your tea," he said. "So, you moved in with your sister. And?"

She tapped her spoon against her cup, and placed it on the saucer. "And after a few years I decided to attend secretary's school at night. I completed the course and eventually found a job. Then I worked my way up in an accounting firm. I started as a typist. And I'm office manager now." She bit into her sandwich, not wanting to talk any more about herself.

"Well, well," mused Brendan. "It sounds like life has been good to you." He held up his sandwich, a hundred questions ready to leap off his tongue. "And is your –"

Mrs. Murphy caught the waiter and asked for a bit of cream for her tea. "And you, Brendan? I heard you had moved, and gotten married, and had done well for yourself," she said brightly.

He stirred some sugar into his tea. "Eventually. Yes. I worked as a machinist in different places.

After Boston, I moved to Baltimore." He took a sip of tea. "Then Harrisburg, and eventually to Philadelphia. Couldn't seem to settle down. Was on the move for years."

She looked away from his piercing eyes, and took the cream offered by the waiter and poured a splash into her tea. Then she took a small bite of her sandwich, and gave a brisk nod for Brendan to continue, as if they were merely discussing the weather.

"Then I met Elizabeth, and stayed put in Philadelphia. Never had a reason to go back to Boston."

Mrs. Murphy brought the cup to her lips, and took a tiny sip. Was he throwing darts her way? Or was it just her own guilt pricking her at every possible opportunity?

"We were married for twenty-five years," Brendan continued. "Elizabeth passed away, oh, over ten years ago."

"I'm so sorry," she said, setting the cup down with a noisy clank as it hit the rim of the saucer.

For a few moments, nothing was said. Mrs. Murphy was revising the history she had made for him; she suddenly felt vulnerable to know that he was no longer married.

"And what about your hus–" Brendan began to ask, but she cut him off.

"Any children?" she asked, refilling their cups.

He leaned back and feigned the same relaxed ease. "One daughter. Nancy. My pride and joy. And four grandchildren, to date." He pulled out his wallet. "And if you don't mind me playing the proud granddad, I'll show you some photographs. That's Angelo, eight – a good lad – wants to be a fireman. This here's Maria, just turned six – the apple of my eye. Brian, five – a handful, that one. And the wee babe, Julia."

"My, my. Darling, all of them. How wonderful for you – and them. They have their own private Santa in you – year round."

"True, true," he laughed. "I have to take care that they don't see my costume. Brian caught me trying it on last year and I had to do a bit of impromptu acting, saying Mrs. Claus sent me early to check out the chimney to make sure I could still fit, blaming my girth on her cooking. Had to make a quick exit out the door, with Brian standing there, his mouth hanging open. Never said a word!" He slapped his thigh, almost slipping into his Santa personality, so heartily did he laugh.

Mrs. Murphy noticed that his brogue was all but gone tonight. As if it had come out unbidden from the past when he had seen her unexpectedly, and was now safely shelved away, along with the long years since.

She laughed at his stories, remembering the delight she had always felt in his company, the bit of magic he effortlessly sprinkled over everything. She remembered that life was always intensified around him, charged with the promise of excitement, adventure. A tiny feeling of jealousy washed over her briefly for the years the lucky woman Elizabeth had with him.

Brendan finished his sandwich and washed it down with a swig of tea. Then he leaned aside, as the waiter cleared their plates. "And what about –"

"This is your daughter? A lovely girl," said Mrs. Murphy, examining the photograph.

"That's my Nancy. And her husband, Guido. I'd hoped she'd marry a fine Irishman, but I couldn't have chosen better myself. He's the best of husbands and fathers. My Nancy couldn't be happier."

He slipped the wallet back into his pocket. "I took to visiting them here for the holidays, after Elizabeth died. Then when the children started coming, I found myself coming more often and staying longer." He laughed and pulled on his beard. "This was all Nancy's idea. I started playing Santa to her little ones, and she convinced me to try the department stores. Said they could use a realistic looking Santa. Said no one looked more like the old fool than me."

"Oh, come now, I'm sure she said no such thing," laughed Mrs. Murphy.

"No. My Nancy would never be cruel."

Mrs. Murphy inwardly flinched, wondering if he was trying to wound her.

But he continued in a light, playful manner. "I had the costume. So I thought, why not? I've enjoyed it over the years. Though by the looks some of the mothers throw at me, I'm afraid I give the little ones too much hope. And you?" he said quickly. "I suppose you have a dozen grandchildren by now?"

Mrs. Murphy leaned back and crossed her hands in front of her. "Nieces and nephews, all with children of their own. Seven great-nieces and -nephews here in New York alone. They keep me quite busy."

"Seven. Well, well. Seven of them." He waited for her to say something more.

"And you've lived in New York for how long, Brendan?" She found herself wanting to say his name; it somehow closed the years between them.

"Two years now. Nancy keeps pestering me to move in with them, or at least to get a place close by." He shifted around in his chair, determined to have an answer to the question that was foremost in his mind. "And you and your husband, where do you live?"

She lifted the teapot and poured, but the pot was empty. She pretended not to notice. "I live alone now."

"Oh, I'm sorry," he said, scanning her face to see if he had caused her any pain.

"Down in Grammercy. A lovely neighborhood, with a park nearby. Beautiful flowers. I often stroll by there when the weather is fine."

He watched her closely, trying to read her face. The conversation shifted briefly to the war, and then to their plans for Christmas. They finished their tea, and Brendan paid the bill.

"Thank you, Brendan. I've enjoyed myself."

"How about a stroll? Do you have the time? We can take in the Christmas decorations. Let's go watch the skaters! Then warm up with a cup of hot cocoa. What do you say? It'll be like old times."

Mrs. Murphy smiled, remembering his contagious enthusiasm. It took her the smallest of moments to break her old habit of saying no to late evenings during the week. "That'd be grand!"

Mrs. Murphy's heart beat in girlish excitement as she took his arm. She hadn't acted so impulsively, she laughed to herself, since – well, since her days with Brendan.

# Chapter 5

Lillian sat at the switchboard, tapping her pencil on the desk, her eyes on the clock. She was looking forward to having lunch with Izzy. Other than a quick hello in the morning, she hadn't seen her friend for a week. Izzy's liveliness and energy had a way of offsetting the more problematic areas of the job. Lillian couldn't help thinking that she should be more like Izzy. More vocal, more assertive. More of a doer.

Izzy had been devastated when Red said he wanted to hold off on their wedding, and though she was always worried about him, she didn't let it get in the way of living. Now here she was, thriving in her new role at Rockwell Publishing: taking charge of the floor, making the schedules for the typists and clerks, taking minutes for Mr. Rockwell, training the new girls. Izzy was sharp, ambitious, professional, and confident. She was the type of woman who made things happen, despite setbacks.

Lillian put on her coat and hat, and waited for Izzy to finish explaining the filing system to one of the new girls.

"Ready?" Izzy asked, and linked her arm with Lillian's as they headed out the door.

All the way to the café, they talked of the war, the rumors, and how quickly everything had changed. Izzy told her that on Monday, the day after Pearl Harbor, the whole city reeled as details of the attack came in.

"You wouldn't believe it, Lilly. Storeowners were throwing out anything that was made in Japan – throwing it right out onto the sidewalks. People were gathered in groups everywhere, trying to figure out what had happened. Everyone found a radio to listen to the President's speech, to the updates – they clustered around cars with the radios blasting, crowded in cafes, shops, everyone exchanging news, trading information. Much of it wrong. Someone said Pearl Harbor was in New Jersey – that set hearts pounding. Someone else said it was hoax, like the *War of the Worlds* – remember that? Others said the German Luftwaffe was on its way here. It was pandemonium. Truly frightening."

Lillian listened to Izzy's account with amazement. "I thought it was bad upstate – it must have been terrible here."

Izzy shook her head. "The world has been turned upside down." She opened the door to the little Italian café they sometimes lunched at. She pointed out the American flag that now hung outside the door, where last week hung an Italian flag.

Lillian whispered to Izzy. "I guess they want us to know whose side they're on."

"Either that, or they don't want to lose any business," said Izzy.

They entered the noisy café and slid into a booth. Lillian immediately noticed a difference from the last time – there was more energy, more tension in the air, more movement. Different levels of conversation mixed with the music of the radio coming from the counter. She immediately picked up on a different attitude towards the Italian owner and waiters. Even though the owner displayed a second American flag by the register, there was a decided change towards him, a wariness that had not existed before.

Lillian greeted the waiter in her usual friendly manner when she placed her order, and saw the woman at the next table shake her head disapprovingly. When the waiter came back with two cups of soup, Lillian smiled, but he seemed angry as he left.

Izzy raised her eyebrows and peered at the soup. "I guess it's safe to eat."

"Oh, Izzy!"

Izzy leaned forward. "I know I shouldn't be happy about anything to do with this war, and I'm not – but they say that a lot of the Americans who joined the RAF want to come home so they can fight against the Japs."

"Does that mean Red will come home?"

"I think there's a good chance. That's all I can think about." For a moment, Izzy was her old self, bursting with enthusiasm and happiness.

"Have you had any word from him?" asked Lillian.

The carefree expression immediately vanished. "Last week. I finally got a letter, longer than the ones he had been sending. It turns out it's more than his leg. I knew he wasn't telling me everything." She looked out the window and narrowed her eyes, as if she were still piecing it all together. "I think maybe he had some sort of breakdown. His letters had practically trickled off to nothing. Then in this letter he told me that two of his buddies had been killed on the same mission that he caught the shrapnel."

"Oh, my God," said Lillian. "How devastating for Red."

"But that was four months ago. Something's not right." She shook off the feeling and started in on her soup, but her brow remained knitted. "He's recovering in the north of England somewhere. In some enormous manor house they've converted into a rest and recovery hospital. He hasn't so much as mentioned our wedding. I guess I can't blame him."

"I hope he comes home soon. For both your sakes." Lillian saw the moment in Izzy's face when she veered close to self-pity, and then decided on a different course of action.

"In the meantime," said Izzy, "I mean to do my part. Make the best of a bad situation." She crumbled some crackers into her soup. "I'm signing up for volunteer work. The options are endless now: air raid wardens, plane spotters, Red Cross work. I know a couple of gals working at the defense centers – the canteens. I'm going with them tonight. Serve coffee and donuts. Hand out paper and pencils to the GIs so they can write home."

"Maybe I can join you some nights. See if Mrs. Kuntzman can babysit the boys. I'd like to do whatever I can." Lillian tasted the minestrone soup. Delicious.

"I need to do something," said Izzy. "I feel like everything is on hold. Every day I check the mail for letters from Red – but he's not much of a writer," she laughed. "I figure maybe I can get some of these guys at the canteen to write to their gals, let them know how they're doing."

Lillian knew that she would feel the same way. Anything was better than just waiting, not knowing what was going on, as she was beginning to feel with Charles.

"You can knit, right?" asked Izzy, putting her spoon down. "The Navy's looking for women to knit socks, turtlenecks, and watch caps."

"That way I could stay at home with the boys," said Lillian, thrilled that there was a way for her to help out. She had felt helpless in the face of the pummeling news reports, and now here was something practical she could do. "Charles was in the Navy, you know."

Izzy looked up. "Do you think he'll rejoin?"

"I don't know," Lillian said. She kept telling herself that he would be too old, but some part of her knew that he was going to serve again, in some capacity. "I'll get some yarn on my way home." The thought of knitting for the sailors made her feel that she would be doing something connected to Charles.

"The worse thing is just to sit and wait," said Izzy. "Not knowing what's going to happen. Thank God for my job! I'm finding that I'm actually good at it, managing the staff."

"Your new role really suits you," said Lillian. "Though Mr. Rockwell has few redeemable qualities, at least he has the good sense to recognize talent when he sees it."

"You know," said Izzy, making room for the waiter to set their sandwiches down. "I think he saw this coming. I mean, not Pearl Harbor, but that war was just a matter of time, and he didn't want to be left short-handed. Little by little he's been promoting the women. For months, now."

Izzy took the toothpick out of her hot pastrami and lifted the sandwich to take a bite. "I have to say, I'm grateful to Mr. Rockwell for giving me the chance. He could have given it to one of the other girls. It's really helped to take my mind off things. And, you know, he's really not as bad as you think."

"If you say so. Though do be careful. I've seen the way he ogles you. Haven't you noticed?"

Izzy shrugged. "The same way he ogles every woman. I guess I've chosen to ignore it. It seems beside the point. I just want to be kept busy. I've come to know him better, and I can see his good qualities." She laughed at the skepticism on Lillian's face. "Well, okay, one or two of them. And even Mr. Weeble improves on closer acquaintance."

"Okay, now you've gone too far," laughed Lillian. "He's been a thorn in my side ever since I started. He's always snooping over my shoulder, trying to catch me in the act of sketching. Ever since he saw the drawing I made of him as a lizard."

"Well, really Lilly, you can hardly blame him. Especially since you so exactly captured his expression."

"I'm sure he was eavesdropping the other day when I was telling you about my portfolio. I always get the feeling he's spying on me."

Izzy took another bite of her sandwich. "Well, you never know why people behave the way they do," she said. "But once he's away from his desk, he's really not so bad. Mr. Rockwell says Weeble can be counted on for anything he throws at him – managing Marketing and Advertising, for example. That's a lot to take on. Rockwell's come to depend on him. Both men have their good points, Lilly."

"Hmm." Lillian would humor Izzy, but she was not prepared to change her opinion. About either man.

Izzy picked up the dill pickle on her plate. "How about you, Lilly? You seem a little," she crunched on the pickle, one eye squeezing shut at the sourness, "I don't know, off."

Lillian took a deep breath and sighed, considering how much to tell Izzy. "Well, I was terrified by the news. Like everyone. And I was disappointed to have to cut our trip short. I miss Annette so much."

"And Charles?" Izzy asked. "I bet they all loved him."

Lillian nodded, remembering their few days upstate. "Annette and Bernie took to him immediately. I could tell that he enjoyed his time at their orchard, being out in the open. He and Bernie had plans to take the boys hiking, to look for their Christmas tree, lots of things. Then the news came." Lillian didn't want to tell Izzy about the disagreement with Charles. She was afraid it would make Izzy think too much of her own postponed wedding.

"And now it feels as though I've never left the switchboard. It's become so monotonous. I really admire the way you're reshaping your job."

"Push ahead, Lilly. Make yourself known. The only women who are getting ahead in the office are the ones who seek out more work, demand a raise, or speak to Mr. Rockwell about redefining their positions. Why don't you talk to him about getting into the Art Department? I'm sure he'd hear you out."

"I don't feel quite ready yet. I'm still working on some drawings," said Lillian, realizing that it sounded like she was always making excuses.

"There's no time like the present, Lilly. Why don't you at least talk to Rockwell?"

Lillian finished her sandwich, briefly imagining asking Rockwell for a transfer. She shook her head at the image that came to mind, and used her napkin to brush the crumbs from her hands.

"I couldn't. I'd hate to ask him for any favor. Besides, he would pick up on my disdain for him. I can't stand the way he shows attentions to the girls whose husbands or beaus are away. I bet he won't put on a uniform and fight. He'll find some way to pull strings, or pay off someone."

"That's ungenerous of you, Lilly. You don't know. Maybe he will join up, now that we're at war."

Lillian's head snapped up at the rebuke. "You're right. I really don't know him at all. Maybe he will."

They paid, slipped on their coats, and left the café. "When I'm angry about other things," said Lillian, "Mr. Rockwell and Mr. Weeble become my default targets. But I'm truly happy that things are working out for you, Izzy. And I'm glad to hear that Mr. Rockwell and Mr. Weeble are not as bad as I've imagined them to be."

Izzy cocked her head at Lillian and laughed. "You? Angry? That's a first. What are you angry about?"

"Well, not angry. Upset. Disappointed. I didn't want to tell you, but we've decided to postpone the wedding."

Izzy stopped, and turned to Lillian, her eyes full of concern. "But why?"

"Well, actually it was Charles who decided. I don't want to wait. But he – I guess he feels the time isn't right. With so much uncertainty now, he wants to wait and see what happens."

Izzy sighed deeply. "I'm sorry, Lilly. I know how that feels. To have decisions made on your behalf. Maybe he'll change his mind."

# Chapter 6

༄

Lillian met the end of the week with a deep sigh of relief that there had been no further attacks. She was glad for the half day on Friday, which allowed her to pick up the boys from school. After a snack of cookies and milk, she let Tommy and Gabriel play outside with the other kids while she prepared dinner. Though she couldn't see them from the kitchen window, she still found herself looking down at the street periodically, just to make sure that everything appeared normal. And she kept the radio on for the latest news updates.

Tommy and Gabriel sat on the steps in front of Mickey's brownstone, watching him trade baseball cards with some of the other boys from the street. Butch, one of the boys from a few blocks over, walked up with a couple of his friends. When they weren't playing baseball, the band of boys liked to play at being GIs, breaking into groups and scouring the neighborhood for the enemy – though the game was mostly an excuse to hang out at the diner afterwards.

Tommy didn't really like Butch or his sidekick, Spider, but they had a good baseball team, the Bulldogs. For most of the summer Butch's Bulldogs were ahead, but slowly Mickey's team, the Redbirds, had caught up with them and were now just one game behind. The weather had been mild, and it looked as if they could finish the season before it got too cold. They worried that because of the war, their parents might force them to postpone the games. So they had all agreed to play on Saturday, no excuses allowed.

"Tomorrow at 2:00," said Butch. "This will clinch our win."

"Yeah, yeah," said Mickey, putting away his cards. "We're ready for you."

"Hey," said Butch. "We're gonna sweep the neighborhood for spies. You guys up for it?"

"Sure," said Mickey. "Same teams?"

"Platoons," corrected Spider.

"Right," said Mickey. "Platoons. Okay, Platoon A – we'll take the Western Front. Platoon B, you guys head south."

"And remember," said Butch. "If you come across any Jerrys or Japs, shoot to kill. No prisoners."

"We'll meet back at base at 1700 hours, sharp," said Mickey.

Spider turned to his leader. "What time is that, Butch?"

Butch took off his cap and swatted Spider on the head. "It's whenever we're finished, ya dope."

"Synchronize your watches, gentlemen," said Tommy. He had heard that in a movie recently and had been using it ever since. Though none of the boys had watches, they all looked down at their wrists and made tiny adjustments. "Ready? Spread out!"

The gang split into two. Platoon B headed one way, Tommy and Mickey with some of Butch's gang headed the other way.

"Keep an eye out for anything suspicious. There are spies everywhere," said Butch. "We'll check out the avenue. You guys check the side streets. We'll meet at the canteen to compare notes."

Tommy and Mickey slinked down the street, darting from car to car, tree to tree. They pressed their backs against buildings, and then peered stealthily around the corner, their right hands tucked inside their jackets, ready to use their carefully concealed weapons.

They briefly followed two elderly gentlemen, after detecting an accent of some sort.

"Could be spies," whispered Tommy.

"Quick! Down here!" cried Mickey. "A good lookout spot."

They crept down a flight of steps that led to a basement apartment, and took their positions behind the railing, guns ready – only to be startled, and then shooed away, by an elderly woman coming out from her apartment.

"Run!" hollered Tommy, the enemy upon them. He dodged a few bullets and covered his head at the exploding grenade right behind them.

The elderly tenant climbed up the basement steps and shook her head at the boys.

After twenty minutes of crisscrossing the neighborhood, Tommy and Mickey ran up to the corner diner.

"What took you so long?" whined Spider. "Come on! I'm thirsty."

They all crowded into a booth and dumped their change onto the table.

"Shell out," said Spider. As usual Spider and Butch had only a few coins. They all pooled their change, and Butch ordered three chocolate malts with six straws.

"Okay," said Mickey, after the waiter brought their drinks. "Who wants to report first?"

One of Butch's men took a quick break from slurping his malt. "All clear on the Western Front. No reports of unusual activity."

Butch snatched his malt from Spider, who was fast draining it, and punched him on the arm. Spider merely rubbed his arm and took another sip.

"We might have found some German spies," said Tommy. "We saw some suspicious looking men who we think were Jerrys trying to pass as locals."

"Yeah," said Mickey. "When they thought no one was looking, they spoke in German, and laughed." He imitated an evil snicker: "Heh, heh, heh!"

"Good work, men," said Butch. "Keep tracking them."

"Spider? What'd you find?" asked Mickey.

"No maybes for me," said Spider, thumping his thumb on his chest. "I found myself a bona fide spy."

All the boys lifted their heads from their malts, their eyes on Spider.

Spider folded his arms on the table and leaned forward, enjoying their complete attention before revealing his information.

"That Dago lady who runs the corner grocery," he began. "She put something under a bench, real sneaky like." He enacted the scene, exaggerating the actions for dramatic effect. "Looked all around. To the left. To the right. Then took a bag from inside her coat and hid it beneath the bench." He took a long, justified slurp from Butch's malt. "She's definitely spying for Mussolini."

"Nah," said Tommy. "That's Mrs. Mancetti. She's not a spy. She was probably giving food to a poor person. She does stuff like that."

"Oh, yeah? Then why was she being so sneaky like?" challenged Spider. "She could be another Mata Hari."

Mickey burst out laughing in disbelief. "Mrs. Mancetti? Mata Hari?"

"You're way off base, Spider," said Tommy. "As usual," he muttered under his breath before taking a sip of his malt.

"Oh, yeah?" asked Spider, pulling a paper bag from inside his jacket. "Well, here's the evidence." He placed the bag firmly on the table.

"You took it?" said Tommy. "That's stealing!"

"Careful!" cried one of Butch's gang as Spider started to open the bag. "It could be booby-trapped. You shouldn't bring it in here, ya fathead!"

"Yeah? What do *you* know?" said Spider. "There's important information in here." He slowly opened the bag, waiting for the curiosity to build.

All the boys crowded around. "Well, what is it?"

They passed the bag around, each one taking a peek, skeptical of the danger that lurked inside, but not wanting to admit it.

Tommy opened the bag, rummaged around, and scoffed. "Two bagels, a chocolate bar, and some lunch meat." He shook his head at Spider. "You call this evidence?"

Spider rolled his eyes and leaned in, sneering at Tommy. "It's in code, ya sap! The problem with you is that you don't know how to *think* like a spy." He tapped his head. "It's not just any lunchmeat. It's braunsweiger," he said, pronouncing the word with an exaggerated guttural accent. He waited for the significance to register with the boys. "German," he explained to some of the blank faces. "And who eats bagels?" He looked from boy to boy, waiting for the obvious.

Mickey shrugged. "We eat bagels."

Spider ignored the comment. "Jews. That's who. Don't you get it? This is a plot to kill two Jews."

Tommy snorted and folded his arms. "How do you know it's not a plot to kill one German?"

Spider ignored that comment, too. "And Mata Hari is the messenger. We have to keep a close watch on her. She's dangerous."

"What about the chocolate bar?" asked Butch.

"I haven't figured that out yet. But I will." He stuffed the bag back inside his jacket. "In the meantime, I'll hold on to the evidence."

"You mean you'll eat the evidence," said Tommy.

"Look," said Spider, shoving a finger into Tommy's chest. "If she's a spy, I'm gonna make sure she pays for it."

Tommy grabbed Spider's spindly finger and twisted it. "You leave her alone," he threatened.

Some of the boys shifted in their seats, uncomfortable with dissention in the ranks.

Spider rubbed his finger, a glare of contempt in his eyes. "Always on the side of the underdog, aren't you?"

"If that was true, I'd be on your side," answered Tommy.

Spider was just about to answer back, when Mickey interrupted and brought things back under control.

"Right," said Mickey. "Well, you work on breaking the chocolate code. We'll continue surveillance of the Krauts." He took a last pull on his straw. "C'mon, men. Let's go."

A noisy slurping went round the table as the boys sucked up the last of the malts, along with a good deal of air. They then piled out of the booth, and ran out of the diner.

Butch and his gang headed home. "Get ready for tomorrow!" taunted Butch. "We're gonna cream you!"

Tommy waved the threat away, and he and Mickey headed off in the opposite direction. They ran all the way home, and then climbed the steps to Mickey's brownstone and sat on the top step, catching their breath.

"We *have* to beat them, tomorrow," said Tommy. "It's our last chance."

"Don't worry. We will," said Mickey.

Tommy suddenly remembered that he was supposed to keep an eye on Gabriel. He raised his head and peered around. "Where's Gabriel and Billy?"

Mickey stood and looked up and down the street. "Here comes my mom, with Billy. I don't see Gabriel."

It was starting to get dark, and Tommy was getting worried. He saw Mrs. Kinney and Billy walking towards them, with bags of groceries in their arms.

Mickey ran down the steps to take the groceries from his mom.

"Hi, Mrs. Kinney," said Tommy. He pulled Billy aside. "Where's Gabe? I thought he was with you."

"He was," said Billy. "But then Mom made me go to the store with her and he didn't want to come. I guess he went home."

Tommy thrust his hands in his pockets and looked up at the streetlights that had just come on. "Yeah, okay. See ya tomorrow, Mickey."

Tommy didn't know whether to go home and hope Gabriel was there, or wait and see if he would show up. He tried to weigh which choice had more chance of getting him in trouble. He couldn't miss the game tomorrow; he just had to defeat Spider. Then, up ahead, he saw Gabriel walking towards him, taking his time, as usual.

Tommy ran up to him. "Hurry up, Gabe! We're gonna be late." He pulled Gabriel by the arm and hurried him up the steps to their brownstone. "Where the heck were you? You were supposed to stay with Billy."

"I was looking for Tiny."

"Jeez, Gabriel! Just because I don't want you to tag along with me all the time doesn't mean you have to make up imaginary friends. I'm getting tired of hearing about Tiny."

"He's not imaginary. He's real," said Gabriel, as they climbed the stairs to the third floor.

Tommy put his hand on the door knob. "Yeah, yeah. Well, don't tell Mom, or she won't let us play outside anymore."

Lillian was setting the table when they entered the apartment. "There you are! I was starting to get worried."

"We were just playing," said Tommy. "What's for dinner?"

"Meatloaf, roasted potatoes, and salad," said Lillian, noting the look of pleasure on their faces. "Go wash up."

When they were all seated, Lillian asked the boys what they had been playing at with Mickey and Billy.

Tommy kicked Gabriel under the table, as he drained his glass of milk, and wiped his mouth. "Oh, just stuff, and Mickey and the guys swapped baseball cards."

Lillian got up to refill Tommy's glass.

"Mommy, what's a Dago?" asked Gabriel.

"Where'd you hear that?" asked Lillian.

"Someone wrote it on the side of Mancetti's store: Dagos go home!"

Lillian frowned. "It's not a nice word. I don't want you to say it."

"It just means Italian, that's all," said Tommy. "Everybody has a name like that: Wop, Kike, Spic, Mick —"

"Tommy!" said Lillian.

"What, Mom?" asked Tommy. "Everybody says it."

"Well, not you. Do you understand?"

Tommy rolled his eyes.

"They're insulting words, Tommy," said Lillian.

"I'm a Yank. Is there anything wrong with that?"

"It's those other words I'm referring to, and you know it."

"Okay, okay," said Tommy, more interested in another helping of potatoes.

"Mommy," said Gabriel. "Mr. Drooms said he would help me with my bird puzzle when we got back from Aunt Annette's. And we've been back a long time."

"Three days isn't long," laughed Lillian. "I'm sure he'll stop by and help you just as soon as he has time. How about we get out some of our decorations tonight? We have to start getting ready for Christmas."

"Can I write my letter to Santa tonight?" asked Gabriel.

"I already know what my letter will say," said Tommy. "I'm gonna ask for a tank and a model airplane, and there's this target-practice game where you shoot down enemy paratroopers." He looked over to make sure Lillian was paying attention.

"I'm going to ask Santa for a wagon and a sled," said Gabriel.

"And one of those map boards," continued Tommy, "with pins for plotting troop movement. Like the one Mickey has. And I want my own radio."

"Yeah, I want my own radio, too. And a dog house," said Gabriel.

The boys kept adding to their lists, remembering that they wanted roller skates and baseball bats, the latest board games, and telescopes. Lillian raised her eyebrows at most of the items, but made a mental note of the things that she might be able to get for them.

Just as she was clearing the table, there was a knock at the door. Gabriel jumped up and ran to open it.

"Hi, Mr. Drooms! Did you come to help with my bird puzzle?"

Lillian walked to the door, happy that he had stopped by. She hated to think that another day might pass without seeing him. She saw that he carried two bundles of firewood and a small pink box that she recognized as coming from the bakery on Broadway.

"What's all this?" she asked.

"What's in the box?" asked Gabriel.

"Chocolate raspberry cake. If that's all right with your mom," he said.

"Perfect timing," she said. "We just finished dinner."

Charles handed the box to Lillian, and held up the bundles of firewood. "I thought it would be nice to have a fire tonight. If you feel like it."

Tommy took the firewood. "I can make the fire. Don't worry, Mom. I learned all about fire safety in school today. Incendiary training."

"I can help too," said Gabriel. "We had an air raid drill today. We had to hide under our desks and cover our heads."

"Like that's gonna help," laughed Tommy.

"It could help if a brick fell. It would land on my desk instead of my head."

"Well, my teacher said we're going to have to build real bomb shelters," said Tommy.

Lillian shifted the subject. "We were just saying that we have to start decorating for Christmas."

"That's right," said Charles. "It's less than two weeks away."

"Hey! Let's get our tree!" said Tommy.

"And hang our stockings!" cried Gabriel. "And put one of those blue stars in our window!"

Lillian stroked Gabriel's hair. "Those aren't for Christmas."

"Yeah," said Tommy. "We learned all about it in school." He turned to Gabriel to explain. "A blue star in the window means a soldier lives there who's in the service, and a gold star means they got killed."

Lillian sighed; it was impossible to avoid the subject of war. It was creeping in everywhere, into her home, into their minds. She liked to think that when she closed her apartment door, she was shutting out the world. But that was becoming more and more impossible to do. She carried the bakery box to the kitchen counter while the boys busied themselves with the firewood.

Charles joined her in the kitchen. "I missed you," he said, kissing her cheek.

"I was hoping you'd stop by," said Lillian. "I stood by the door last night and waited for you to knock."

Charles laughed and folded her in his arms. "Why didn't you just open the door? When you didn't, I thought you were still angry with me."

"I am still angry with you," Lillian said. "But I still want to see you." She started to cut the cake into slices. "So what made you stop by tonight?"

"Something Mrs. Murphy said as she was leaving the office."

"Mrs. Murphy?" Lillian asked, surprised at his response.

"Yes. According to Mason, she's reconnected with an old friend. At least that's the answer she gave him. He saw her twice with an older gentleman, and asked her who he was." Charles sampled a bite of cake. "I think maybe there was something between them once."

"Really? I've never heard you mention anyone. Not even her husband."

"She's never spoken about her private life. I always got the impression she didn't want to talk about him." He passed the plates to Lillian as she sliced the cake. "When she left tonight, I heard Mason ask her, 'And where are you off to in such a hurry?' She simply smiled and said, 'There's life to be lived, Mr. Mason.' And I thought, she's right. So I stopped off at Buttercup's and bought the cake. Chocolate raspberry."

"My favorite," said Lillian, pleased that he remembered.

They carried the plates to the coffee table, and in between bites, Charles helped Tommy get a small fire going, while Gabriel opened the puzzle box and searched for pieces with straight edges. Lillian looked at the three of them together – at that moment, there was nothing else that she wanted. This was the vision that she had held in her mind for so long – simple evenings at home, small daily pleasures.

The fire burned brightly as they listened to music from the radio. An outline of the puzzle was starting to take shape on the coffee table as Charles helped Gabriel with the pieces. Tommy usually didn't like to work puzzles with Gabriel, but having Charles there made it a more interesting pastime and Tommy soon became absorbed in finding pieces. It wasn't long before they had the borders completed and much of the sky filled in.

Lillian gave in when first Tommy, and then Gabriel, asked for another piece of cake. She went to the kitchen and came back with more slices for them all.

After a few moments, Gabriel looked up. "Mommy, can I save a piece of cake for Tiny?"

"Who's Tiny?" asked Charles.

"Gabriel's new friend," Tommy answered with a laugh.

Charles glanced at Lillian, and then asked Gabriel, "You mean – a little boy?"

"He's more like a boy-man," answered Gabriel.

Charles found a few blue sky pieces with birds in flight and handed them to Gabriel. "And what's Tiny's last name?"

"Tomorrow," answered Gabriel, trying to fit a blue piece near the tree tops, then putting it back and trying another.

"Tiny Tomorrow?" asked Tommy. Slowly the pressure built in his puffed up cheeks, and he burst out laughing, burying his face in his shirt and rolling back against the couch.

"Okay, you two," said Lillian. "Time for bed. Go brush your teeth and get your pajamas on. You can read in bed a while."

Tommy jumped up, still laughing. "Night, Mr. Drooms. Thanks for the cake!"

"Just one more," said Gabriel, with a puzzle piece in his hand. "I have to find where this goes."

Charles pointed to where they had just pieced together a flock of birds. "Maybe somewhere up in here."

Gabriel twisted his body and turned the piece around and around. "I found it!" he said, setting it in place. "Thanks, Mr. Drooms," he said, running off to the bathroom.

Charles took a seat next to Lillian on the couch. "Tiny Tomorrow?"

Lillian leaned against Charles, glad to have a few moments alone with him. "His imaginary friend. I guess it's one of the ways he's dealing with the war and all the changes. He never spoke of him until we were on the train, coming back."

"The war will change everything," said Charles. He gestured to the glowing embers. "Even this. All fuel will have to go to the war effort. Rations are sure to follow soon." He leaned back and put an arm around Lillian. "I thought we should enjoy what we have, while we have it."

They sat quietly for a few minutes, enjoying the peacefulness of the evening. Lillian wondered if such evenings were going to change, along with everything else. She supposed so, and felt sad at the coming loss. But more than anything, she wanted assurance that nothing had changed between her and Charles.

"Izzy finally had a letter from Red. It took him four months to tell her that two of his crew were killed on the same mission that he was wounded. He said he's recuperating and is being looked after. Not to worry. She's hoping that he might come back home."

Charles nodded and continued to stare into the fire.

"At least she has some explanation for why he's been so distant. You never know how the fighting will affect someone. Like you said, war changes people."

He caught the shift in her tone and turned to her. "Is that what you're afraid of?" he asked. "That I'll change?"

"It could happen. All I know is that it would have been easier for Izzy if they had married. She feels like she's being kept at a distance, her life separated from his."

"Maybe that's how he's coping."

"But think how she feels. She feels as alone as he does. They need each other now. There would be some comfort in knowing that they were waiting for each other, that they were in this together."

"That's true. But imagine the thoughts running through his mind. Who knows how many more missions he will have to fly, what might happen to him."

Charles got up and stood by the fire, took up the poker and moved the logs around.

Lillian watched him as he stood there with his hand on the mantel, gazing into the fire. "What is it, Charles?"

He waited a few moments before responding. "I wanted to tell you earlier. I re-enlisted. A few days ago," he said, turning to her.

"Aren't you too old?" asked Lillian, a jolt of fear shooting through her.

"I was an officer," he said simply.

Lillian shifted her fear to anger that he hadn't told her right away. "Why didn't you tell me? Is there anything else you're not telling me?"

"No. I wanted to tell you, but...," his words drifted away.

"But what?"

"I don't know. I'm still getting used to the idea myself. I didn't want to upset you, so soon after all the news. You're not angry, are you?"

"That you signed up? Of course not. How could I be? I'm just – disappointed that things aren't the way I thought they were. I thought we were more open with each other."

He sat down next to her and took her hand. "Nothing has changed."

But something had changed. He was excluding her in decisions that should be theirs, as a couple. First the wedding, now this. She realized that he still thought of them as two individuals, while she thought of them as a couple. He was drifting farther and farther away.

# Chapter 7

∽

On Saturday, Tommy and Gabriel gathered their gear for the ballgame, and stopped by to pick up Mickey and Billy. Mickey was already outside waiting for them, along with most of the Redbirds.

Gabriel sought out Billy among the group of boys but didn't see him. "Where's Billy?" he asked Mickey. Tommy also looked around for him, and anxiously awaited Mickey's response.

"He's got a cold. Mom won't let him go outside today," said Mickey.

Tommy stifled a groan. When Billy was around, Gabriel stayed close by and helped with the ballgame, but when Gabriel was on his own, he tended to wander away. Now he would have the responsibility of keeping track of him. "Stay close this time, Gabriel. Don't make me go searching for you, like last time."

The boys crossed over to Central Park and found the Bulldogs already there, warming up. The larger fields were always in use, so the two teams had taken to playing in a grassy plot just inside the park, across from the lake.

Gabriel kept looking around, as if he was expecting someone. After the first inning, he ran up to Tommy. "I'm just going over to that gazebo to see if Tiny is there."

"Tiny Tomorrow?" laughed Tommy. He mussed Gabriel's hair. "You goofball." The boys were hollering at Tommy to take his position. "Well, stay where I can see you."

"Okay," said Gabriel, and he ran off to the gazebo where he had met Tiny three weeks earlier.

Tiny and his older brother had moved to the neighborhood a few months ago. Gabriel had first spotted Tiny near the lake, a small figure picking up sticks and stuffing them into an old bag. Since he seemed to be on his own, Gabriel had wandered over and befriended him.

On first glance, from a distance, Gabriel had guessed Tiny to be a boy his own age, or maybe eight or nine. But the closer he got to Tiny, the older he seemed to become. He was a thin, waif-like boy dressed in a threadbare black jacket and a black cap, with the type of physique that suggested either wispy boyhood or aged frailty. He was an odd combination of youth and old age; enthusiasm and weariness took turns on his face, bouncing his age all over the place. Gabriel had decided that he was simply an in-between person. He had seen Tiny several times since then, mostly in the park by the gazebo, and sometimes outside Mancetti's store, or helping out the newspaper vendor.

Gabriel now ran over to the gazebo, and was delighted to see Tiny down by the lake. He was there with his old black bag slung over his shoulder, gathering twigs.

"Hi, Tiny!" Gabriel called out.

"Hiya, Gabriel." Tiny spotted a small branch and bent to pick it up; he snapped it into pieces, and tossed them in the bag.

"Picking up sticks for your stove? Can I help?" Gabriel started to search for twigs. "I have a whole bag of sticks for you, Tiny. I got them up at my aunt's. I told you all about it, but then I couldn't find you."

"Thanks, pal." Tiny leaned against the gazebo and gazed out at the lake, suddenly looking very old. "I haven't been out much this week. My brother is sick again." He picked a leaf off a nearby bush and studied it briefly before dropping it to the ground. "He's really sick this time."

"Why don't you call a doctor?" asked Gabriel.

Tiny snatched up a flat rock near his foot and picked a spot out on the lake. Then he leaned to his side, and threw the stone in a horizontal toss, trying to skip it across the water. It plunked into the water with barely a ripple. "I never could do that." He searched for another rock and tried again, throwing with a little more force this time. The rock went straight down. He kicked at the leaves on his way back to the gazebo, and sat on the rough-hewn bench inside.

"What's wrong with him?" asked Gabriel, sitting next to Tiny.

"He has a weak chest. Especially when it gets cold. He was sick every single winter in the orphanage." Tiny's face shifted and became younger. "But the nuns took care of us there. They made sure we were warm, and did their best to keep us healthy and strong. Every winter we lined up at recess, and waited our turn for the honey. They dipped a big wooden spoon into a bucket of honey, and gave each one of us a spoonful. And we just prayed that we would be lucky enough to get a piece of the beeswax. Chew it all day long." A few years left Tiny's face as he remembered the chewy honeycomb.

"The nuns read to us, and sat with my brother when he was sick. Brought in a doctor when he was really sick. And cooked for us." He leaned back on the bench and pulled his knees up, revealing bony white ankles. "Sister Mary Cecelia. Nobody could make chicken soup like her. Nobody." He smacked his lips and swallowed, as if getting a taste right there.

"My mom makes good soup," said Gabriel.

"And Sister Rosetta. The best biscuits you could ever imagine. I used to work in the bakery with her – that was before the laundry. And I can tell you, when those biscuits came fresh out of the oven…" Tiny sighed, smiling at the memory.

"Hey! Why don't you go back there?" asked Gabriel. "Maybe they'll get some soup for your brother."

The youth left Tiny's face and he became around fifty or so now. "Nah. We can't. You have to leave after the eighth grade. When my brother left, I left with him." He stood up and searched the ground outside of the gazebo. "You can't stay there forever, Gabriel. They have to make room for the new kids. They even take babies."

Tiny rubbed his shoe back and forth over something in the dirt, and bent to pick up a foiled gum wrapper. He inspected it, and tossed it in his bag. Then he gazed up at the sky between the bare branches while he calculated the time since leaving the orphanage. "That was – two years and four months ago."

His eyes sharpened, catching a glimpse of something near the base of a bush growing alongside the gazebo. In one quick, agile movement he dropped, lay on his stomach, and reached underneath the gazebo. He pulled out an old, yellowed newspaper. He stood up and brushed himself off. "Good kindling," he said, waving the newspaper, and added it to his bag.

"How long did you live at the orphanage?"

"Not sure exactly. Brother says we arrived in short pants and left in long pants. We were fourteen and eleven when we left. Plenty old to find work. That's the main thing. Between the two of us, we have all kinds of experience: laundry work, bakery work, running errands, sweeping floors, selling newspapers, hauling things. We even ran a popcorn stand last summer. We can always find work." Tiny now became a grown man giving much needed advice to a youngster. "Don't wait too long to get some experience, Gabriel. You never know what's up ahead."

"Okay," said Gabriel, briefly wondering where he should start. He imagined himself tending a popcorn stand, scooping up some hot, fresh popcorn to eat whenever he got hungry. Or maybe he would enjoy bakery or laundry work. He was impressed with all the places Tiny the boy-man had worked. "What'd you do in the laundry?"

"Not much," Tiny said, sitting down again. "Helped Sister Cunagunda fold towels, mostly. Match up socks. It was easy. I liked it down there. It was always warm. Kinda cozy. And always smelled like soap."

He leaned back, remembering. "She was one of my favorites. She used to tell me stories about when she was a kid. She was an orphan, like us. Diphtheria got her whole family. 'Don't look back,' she used to say. 'That'll just cause you to stumble.'" Tiny pointed his finger in front of him, to the future. "This is the direction we all move in, so we might as well look forward. Try to remember that, Gabriel."

"Okay. I will."

Tiny leaped up onto the gazebo bench and squinted into the shrubbery. His face brightened as he spotted some fallen branches inside the brambles. He jumped down and tapped Gabriel on the arm. "Jackpot!" He became ten years old now as he twisted his way in between the bushes.

Gabriel followed him and watched as Tiny began breaking the branches apart, using his foot to steady the thicker ones while he snapped them in two.

Tiny pulled over a large branch. "Man, oh man! This will last all week!" He tried to pull the branch apart at the fork, but it wouldn't break.

Gabriel knelt down on the branch and dug his fingers around it, leaving the smaller limb sticking up. "Okay. Now, Tiny!"

Tiny gave it one or two tugs, and then practically hung from the branch as he put all his weight on it. But the branch didn't budge. Then he decided he would try to jump on the smaller limb to get it to break. They repositioned the branch, with Gabriel kneeling firmly on the thicker part. Tiny took a few steps back.

"Okay, Gabriel. Hold it tight. One. Two. Three!"

Tiny ran and jumped on the smaller limb that was sticking up off the ground. The branch snapped in two, catapulting Gabriel off the limb, and causing Tiny to land backwards on his seat. He and Gabriel opened their mouths wide in surprise, and then burst out laughing, rolling in the leaves, two seven-year-olds doubled over in stitches. They fell on their backs, holding their stomachs, the blue sky and bare trees above them blurring and shaking, as if in on the fun.

"Your face –" Tiny pointed to Gabriel, barely getting out his words. "Your face when –" he started, and crumpled into hilarity.

"I went flying!" said Gabriel, "and you – you –" he burst into laughter again.

Their laughter slowly wound down. Tiny sat up, cough laughing, and wiped the tears from his eyes.

"Gabriel!" came Tommy's voice from the ballgame.

Gabriel rolled over onto his elbows. "That's Tommy. I gotta go." He stood up and brushed the leaves off his clothes. "Hey, how about I bring the bag of sticks to your home?"

"That'd be swell, Gabriel. Then you can meet my brother." Tiny stood and used his cap to swat away the leaves on his pants and jacket.

"Do you want me to bring some soup for your brother?"

"Nah. I have money from my jobs." He spotted a wadded up paper sack under some brambles and reached in for it, and then tossed it into his bag. "And Mrs. Mancetti gives me food sometimes. I used to do jobs for her – sweep the store, take out the trash. But Mr. Mancetti told me to beat it. I still stick around, just in case she needs something. I had to wash off some graffiti for her yesterday. She puts the food under the bench for me. Could be a bologna sandwich or a box of crackers. Sometimes there's even a chocolate bar."

"Gabriel!" came Tommy's voice again, more urgent now.

"Gotta go. See ya, Tiny!" Gabriel ran ten steps, and then ran back. "Hey, Tiny! You think *I* could run a popcorn stand?"

"Sure. When you're a little older. If I'm still around, I'll help you out. Show you the ropes."

"Gee! That'd be swell! Bye, Tiny!" he hollered as he ran off.

"So long, Gabriel." Tiny hoisted the bag of sticks onto his shoulders, and made his way out of the park, a seventy-year-old man calling it quits for the day.

Tommy stood in the makeshift ball park, punching his baseball glove. "Where the heck were you? Hurry up, Gabe! We need you to field. One of the guys had to leave. Go get your glove!"

Gabriel ran to the far end of the grassy stretch, and chased the balls that were hit his way. He watched Tommy and punched his glove, like Tommy did, and threw his arms up in exaggerated disappointment, just like Tommy, when one of the guys from the Bulldogs got a hit. But the Redbirds were winning, five to four.

The lamplights came on just as the ninth inning was wrapping up. The Redbirds whooped as they struck out the last player and won the game, evening up the games with the Bulldogs.

"Tie-breaker next week," hollered Butch.

"Get ready to weep," added Spider. "We won't go so easy on you next time."

The two teams exchanged a few other taunts as they said their goodbyes and scattered for home.

Tommy and Gabriel ran up the stairs, burst into the apartment, and tossed their coats onto the hall tree, and their baseball gloves on the floor. They headed straight for the table, where the aroma of fried chicken made them suddenly ravenous with hunger.

"Oh no, you don't," said Lillian. "Go wash up first."

Tommy ran to the bathroom, and recounted the high points of the game over the sound of the running faucet. "And then the pitcher tried to throw a curve ball and I slammed it! I hit in the winning run! Did you see that, Gabe?" he hollered.

Lillian took Gabriel's hands and turned them over, examining the dirty nails and palms. "Gabriel! How did you get your hands so dirty? Come here." She lifted him to the kitchen counter and soaped up his hands, and then scrubbed them over the sink with the nail brush.

"I was picking up sticks with Tiny."

"More sticks?" She dried his hands, and then lifted him down. "I thought you had more than enough from Annette's."

Tommy ran back to his seat and lifted his plate. "I'm starving!"

Lillian filled their plates with chicken, peas, and mashed potatoes. "So what does Tiny do with all these sticks, Gabriel? Does he build things?"

"Yeah," said Tommy. "Flying machines to the moon."

"He burns them in the stove," said Gabriel. "To keep warm."

Tommy put his fork down loudly. "Gabriel, imaginary people don't feel the cold. They don't need fuel."

"He's not imaginary."

"Oh, yeah? So where does he live? What does he do all day?" challenged Tommy.

"He lives around here. He works for the newspaper man. And sometimes at Mancetti's. But mostly he just collects free things."

Tommy started to laugh, but Lillian gave him a quick shake of her head.

"What kind of free things?" asked Lillian, thinking that perhaps she hadn't been paying enough attention to Gabriel. Maybe there was something he wanted or was worried about.

"Gum wrappers. Old newspapers. Sticks."

"Only free things?" she asked.

"Yeah. The nuns told him it's better to work for your keep."

Lillian stopped eating and looked carefully at Gabriel. "What nuns?"

"At the orphanage. That's where they used to live."

Lillian set down her knife and fork. "Tommy, who has Gabriel been talking to?"

"No one. I don't know," said Tommy. "Some cousin was visiting Butch. Maybe he was talking, I don't know."

"Are you watching him all the time when you play outside?"

"Yeah, Mom. Gabriel was playing baseball with us, weren't you, Gabe?"

"Yeah, I was a catcher, Mom," said Gabriel.

"A fielder," corrected Tommy.

"Yeah, I was a fielder and chased the ball and threw it back."

Lillian gave a little shake of her head and laughed. She watched Tommy take a second helping of everything. "I don't know where you put all that food, Tommy."

*

After dinner, Lillian read the newspaper while Gabriel worked on his bird puzzle and Tommy stretched out on the couch reading the *Hardy Boys*, biting his nails in suspense.

Her mind was scattered: on Charles, on the frustration with her job, on what she could buy the boys for Christmas. But an article on the 1939 World's Fair caught her attention, and the accompanying photograph of the futuristic buildings tugged at her heart. In a flash, she was back in her old apartment in Brooklyn, at a turning point in her life.

Lillian often felt that her life had begun to change that year, starting with an advertisement for telephone operators for the World's Fair. Apparently, they were going to need an army of operators, and training would be provided. After a lonely period in her life of struggle and despair, a window had suddenly opened, offering her a chance at something new. She nervously applied for the job, and was shocked when she was hired on the spot. She had only been able to work there for the summer, while the boys were out of school, but it had provided the necessary experience for her to later be hired by Rockwell Publishing. And that, too, she hoped, was just a stepping stone to a different job. Her life had slowly started to take shape, and she had begun to live again, after several difficult years of widowhood.

The World's Fair. It had all seemed so momentous, so promising. She remembered how strange the architecture had seemed to her at first. "The World of Tomorrow" was the theme. Everything was new and forward looking and modern. The first time she visited the Fair, she had felt apprehensive of the sleek shapes, the extraordinary technology, the masses of people. It made her realize that at heart she was just an old-fashioned country girl.

But she had adjusted to the crowds, the people from faraway places, the busy pace, the futuristic exhibits almost too far-fetched to believe – television, washing machines, air-conditioning, electric typewriters, and other inventions that were sure to make life easier in the future. Even something as simple as stockings. She had been skeptical of the DuPont display of nylons, but within a year, all the women were wearing them, couldn't live without them.

How much the world had changed since then, she thought. All the goodwill and friendship between countries, the hope for a brighter future, had crumbled away.

She gave a small cry of disappointment on reading that the remaining buildings, including the Japanese pavilion, were being demolished.

"What, Mom?" asked Tommy, looking up from his book.

"It says here that they're tearing down the last of the buildings from the World's Fair."

"Aww shucks!" said Gabriel. "I wanted to go back there." He walked on his knees to her side and looked at the photograph of the stark white spire and sphere.

"Hey, Tommy," said Gabriel, going back to his puzzle, "remember Elektro, the smoking robot?" He imitated the stiff metal man.

"Remember the roller coaster?" asked Tommy. "Remember Futurama?"

Gabriel jumped up, arms stretched out in front of him. "And Superman?"

The boys recounted all the things they had seen, surprising Lillian that they remembered so much. For her, it was the foreign pavilions that most fascinated; the World's Fair was the closest she had ever come to traveling.

But what made the greatest impression on her was the "Masterpieces of Art" building. She had stood mesmerized in front of the works by Michelangelo, da Vinci, and Rembrandt, deeply moved by what could be expressed by the human mind and hand. She had gone back again and again to stand in front of Vermeer's *The Milkmaid* – awed by the alluring blue of the maid's apron, the points of light on the basket and crust of bread, the enigmatic expression on the young woman's face, the illuminating wash of sunlight. Lillian had resonated deeply with the artist who so lovingly and brilliantly elevated the humble to the exquisite. She had determined to work and work and work on her own skills so that she could better express the love she felt for the small, the ordinary, the beautiful in the day to day.

She leaned back on the couch, wondering why she had stopped with her plans. She had accomplished so much in two short years: moving to Manhattan, finding a new job, starting a life with Charles. And now she found herself at a standstill. She had expanded her portfolio and had worked hard at improving her skills. What was preventing her from taking the next step towards her dream, and taking her portfolio around?

She knew full well what it was, and felt cowed by the memory. It still smarted every time she replayed the one time she had taken her portfolio to a magazine office, back in the spring. She had been so determined to make a go of it, had felt so prepared. She had taken the day off to stop by a few design firms and magazine offices. At the first place, she had tentatively knocked on the office door and was told to take a seat. After an hour, she got up the courage to ask the receptionist if it would be much longer; she thought they had perhaps forgotten about her. Half an hour later, she was shown into an office full of people running around, arguing over drawings, phones ringing. The receptionist took her to a crowded desk and left her there.

The man behind the desk was just getting off the phone and jotting something down. He reached his hand over the mounds of papers on his desk, without even looking up at Lillian. "Your portfolio?" was all he said.

She hadn't brought it with her. She stood there mute, feeling like a schoolgirl. He finally lifted his head, raised his eyebrows at her, and poked his head forward waiting for an answer. She had stuttered out a long-winded excuse that she didn't have it with her because she thought she should first come to inquire whether they were actually interested in perhaps seeing her work.

The man had shaken his head, gone back to his papers, and told her to come back when she was ready. That he didn't appreciate people wasting his time.

She had gone back home feeling defeated, and decided to wait until she was more prepared.

Her brow furrowed as she realized that she was even less prepared now; the time was not right. The whole world was at war. Her plans with Charles were shifting with each day. She didn't know what lay ahead in the coming weeks, or what the following year would bring.

No, she thought, folding the newspaper. Now was not the time to start showing her portfolio. Perhaps in the spring. Or summer. Perhaps next year.

# Chapter 8

❧

Lillian mechanically answered the lights at the switchboard, her mind crowded with worries and fears. The news had been trickling in about the attack on Pearl Harbor: the death toll was over two thousand, the Navy was in shambles. The sense of vulnerability and shock hit her for a second time, this time more slowly and methodically as the details emerged.

And now she had the additional burden of knowing that Charles had enlisted. She told herself that because he was past the draft age of forty-five, though only by a year, he would be stationed in the States. But she knew him well enough to know that he would go wherever he was needed. Until that time came, she wanted them to be married, to begin their life as a couple.

She used to feel that she could discuss anything with Charles, but his change of heart about their wedding plans had left her feeling alone with her fears and concerns. She didn't want to burden her sister with her problems; Annette had worries of her own. And Lillian felt that she couldn't talk to Izzy about her fears for Charles, with Red lying wounded.

However, as far as work issues, Lillian and Izzy were always there for one another, and frequently vented their aggravations to each other. Izzy appreciated Lillian's clear-sighted advice, and Izzy's cheerful disposition had a way of recasting Lillian's problems into manageable challenges. So Lillian hadn't given it much thought when, earlier in the day, she said something off-hand to Izzy about being bored with the switchboard.

But Izzy clearly didn't want to hear it. For the first time, Lillian regretted having expressed her feelings to Izzy. She had noticed a change in Izzy the past few days, a kind of distance, and assumed it came from some temporary upset. But today Izzy was being decidedly cold to her.

Lillian searched for an explanation for the change in her behavior. True, Izzy was busier than ever. The attack on Pearl Harbor and the subsequent declarations of war had resulted in nearly all the young men at Rockwell Publishing enlisting, and Izzy was in charge of much of the rescheduling and reassignment of duties. Izzy was extremely organized and efficient, but Lillian worried that she was spreading herself too thin, taking on too much. She was beginning to exhibit behavior that concerned Lillian. Izzy was becoming abrupt and authoritative in her new role. Earlier in the day, Lillian had come upon one of the new girls crying in the bathroom, after Izzy had snapped at her. Lillian tried to comfort the girl, saying that the war was making everyone tense, and that Izzy was a kind and generous person, but was under a heavy work load just now.

Rather than speculate what might be wrong, Lillian decided to speak to Izzy about it. At the end of the day, Lillian stopped by Izzy's desk before leaving.

"Can I talk to you, Izzy?"

One of the girls came by with an invoice for Izzy to sign. "Sure," Izzy answered. She briefly glanced over the numbers, signed, and returned it to the girl, never lifting her eyes to Lillian.

"Is everything all right, Izzy?"

"Yes. Wonderful. Why?" Three flat words that in effect told Lillian to mind her own business.

"Well, I'm wondering if you're not getting overworked. You seem awfully – preoccupied – these past few days."

Izzy simply shrugged, obviously not wanting to talk about it.

"I know you're under a lot of pressure Izzy, but some of these girls aren't used to such a fast-paced environment. After you chastised the new girl, I came across her crying in the powder room."

Izzy's mouth tightened, but she remained silent.

Lillian tried to ease the mood and laughed lightly. "She reminded me of myself when I first started – unsure of what was what, trying to do a good job, but not really knowing what was expected of me."

"It's for her own good," said Izzy, with an edge to her voice. "She needs to toughen up. And so do you, Lilly."

The tables had suddenly turned. "What do you mean?" asked Lillian, feeling her cheeks heat up. This was not intended to be a conversation about her.

"I've told you and told you to speak to Mr. Rockwell about moving to the Art Department. You complain about your job but don't do anything about it. Opportunity isn't going to come running up to you, Lilly. You have to go out and seize it. I told you I would speak to him for you, but you said no. What more do you want?"

"I can speak for myself. And I will. When I'm ready." Lillian was aware of sounding defensive, but Izzy had never spoken to her like this before.

"Let's not argue, Lilly. I'll see you tomorrow."
Izzy got up and went to the file cabinets.

*

Lillian rode the bus home, feeling drained and dispirited. She gazed out the window and noted the holiday decorations in the store windows and along the avenue, but she felt no connection to the Christmas season. It seemed almost a chore to her, all the things that still needed to be done. The holiday spirit seemed to elude her this year. No wonder, she thought, as she passed an enlistment station with a long line of young men waiting to sign up. In less than two weeks, everything had changed.

When she arrived home with the boys, she was surprised to see Charles looking out his door, as if he had been waiting for them.

"Hi, Mr. Drooms!" cried Tommy and Gabriel.

He walked over to them, and his expression seemed to change on seeing Lillian. She wondered if she appeared as disheartened as she felt.

"Do the boys have homework tonight?" asked Charles.

"No! Why?" asked Tommy, sensing something fun about to be suggested.

"Well," said Charles, "I thought we could get our Christmas tree tonight."

A little spark flickered inside Lillian. He said *our* Christmas tree, she thought. One simple word shouldn't have such power over me. And yet it does.

The boys jumped at the possibility of an outing on a school night. "Can we Mom, please?" asked Tommy. "You said we should start on our Christmas decorations."

"You haven't had dinner yet," said Lillian, trying to think what she could quickly put together.

Charles put a hand on her shoulder. "Why don't I take them to the diner for a bite?" he suggested. "Then we'll go to the Christmas tree lot. Give you a couple of hours to relax."

Did he somehow know that she needed some time to herself? She looked down at the boys.

"Please, please, please?" said Gabriel, his hands folded in hope.

"Can we, Mom?" asked Tommy.

"All right," she smiled.

"I'll just get my coat." Charles quickly ducked into his apartment and came back out. "Can we bring anything back for you?"

Lillian shook her head.

"We'll be back soon," he called out, as the boys clamored down the stairs.

Lillian took off her hat and coat and stepped out of her shoes, relieved that she didn't have to worry about dinner. And she was glad that Charles was taking care of getting the tree; that was one thing off her list. She could use the evening to fill the boys' stockings. Perhaps she could even have them hanging by the time they returned.

She made a quick meal for herself, and then went to her bedroom and took a bag from the back of her closet. She sat on her bed and emptied out all the little gifts and goodies she had been collecting: games of jacks and bags of marbles, dominos for Tommy, pick-up sticks for Gabriel, and two comic books each: *The Lone Ranger* and *Red Ryder* for Gabriel, who loved Westerns, and for Tommy, two comic books featuring the new action hero he was so taken with, *Captain America*.

She spread out the assorted candies, where their tastes also diverged, and separated them into two different piles. For Tommy: red hots, lemon drops, hard sour balls. And for Gabriel: taffy, lollipops, licorice. She smiled and thought how the candy reflected their temperaments. Tommy tended to make snap judgments, liked decisive action, quick results. Gabriel tended to ponder over matters, weigh things out. Was much more of a dreamer, like herself. Tommy was more like his father. She was sure Tommy would carve out his place in the world, and succeed at whatever he put his mind to. But she sometimes worried about Gabriel. Perhaps it was because he was still so young that he seemed so vulnerable.

She made a strong cup of tea and sipped it as she wrapped the tiny presents. When she was all done, she felt somewhat revived. She hung the stockings on the mantel, and arranged the Christmas cards behind them. Who knows, she thought, things could be quite different this time next year. She would try her best to make this a good Christmas.

While she waited for Charles and the boys to come home, Lillian took out the boxes of Christmas tree lights and ornaments. She found some Christmas music on the radio, and began to unpack the decorations. She was just untangling the lights and winding them in large coils, when Charles and the boys returned with the tree.

Gabriel ran in first and held the door open, while Tommy and Charles maneuvered the tree through the door and set it in the living room. The boys immediately spotted the stuffed stockings hanging from the mantel.

"Our stockings!" they cried, running to the fireplace.

Lillian inhaled the pine scent and walked over to admire the tree. "Oh, it's beautiful!" she said.

Tommy and Gabriel felt the tiny gifts in their stockings and tried to determine what they might be. Their excitement filled the apartment, and Lillian found herself and Charles laughing at some of their guesses.

While Charles and Tommy set up the tree and strung the lights, she fixed a plate of cookies and Christmas candy for them all, and turned up the volume on the radio. She carefully unpacked the ornaments, and they all began to hang them. Finally, she thought, the Christmas spirit had entered their home.

Gabriel put a hook into a glass ornament, a red-uniformed nutcracker. "Mommy, do legs grow back?"

Lillian stopped and looked from Gabriel to Charles.

"There was a wounded soldier outside the Christmas tree lot," Charles said softly.

"Yeah," said Tommy. "He was sitting on a board with wheels and scooted himself around with his hands."

"Will his legs grow back?" asked Gabriel.

Lillian took a deep breath. "No, honey. But maybe he'll learn to walk with artificial legs, or crutches."

"Oh." Gabriel took another ornament, a tiny drum, and hung it next to the soldier.

Lillian wanted to take their minds off any talk of the war. After hanging a few more ornaments, she clasped her hands. "Guess what I was thinking we could do this weekend?"

Both boys snapped to attention and waited for her to finish. Gabriel already had his mouth open and his eyes wide in anticipation.

"What?" asked Tommy.

"How about we see a matinee? *Dumbo*!"

"Yippee!" cried Gabriel. "Billy said it's great!"

"*Dumbo*?" said Tommy, disappointed.

"Sure. How about we all go?" asked Charles. "Get some popcorn."

"And Milk Duds," added Tommy, suddenly changing his mind about the outing.

Lillian curled up on the couch and watched Charles, laughing as the boys instructed him on where to hang the ornaments. He always knew exactly what she wanted, was always there to help her out. On nights like this, with all of them together, Lillian liked to think that they were already a real family, enjoying each other's company, and making plans for the future.

Such a scene usually flooded her with happiness. But now she wondered if they were ever going to be a family, if Charles was ever going to be her husband. The war could last for years, with an uncertain outcome. She feared that if they didn't marry soon, they might never have the chance again. The idea of almost having something so beautiful, and then seeing it drift away, filled her with a deep sense of loss. She hated the war for all the death and sorrow it had caused, and for filling everyone with fear. And she hated it for coming between her and Charles.

# Chapter 9

෧

Lillian purposely didn't pack her lunch the next day so that she could meet Izzy for lunch. She couldn't stand having anything between them. She would speak to her about it, clear the air.

She passed Izzy's desk on her way in. "Morning, Izzy!" she said as brightly as she could muster. "How about lunch today?"

"Not today, Lilly. I have plans. Sorry." It was the tone that was unlike Izzy. Cold. Distant. And she barely looked up from the folders she was sorting on her desk.

"Oh. Another time, then." Lillian went back to the busy switchboard and felt like she was slowly being deserted. First by Charles. Now by Izzy. Was it something in herself? she began to wonder.

All morning Lillian answered the non-stop lights of the calls, wondering how a job could be both stressful and boring at the same time. She had taken out her sketchbook to draw between calls, as she usually did, but the calls were unrelenting and didn't allow for anything more than a few scribbles of chaotic lines and shapes.

When the lunch hour came, Lillian decided to get a quick bite, and then go for a walk. It would help to clear her head. She left the switchboard room – and her mouth dropped open. There was Mr. Rockwell helping Izzy on with her coat. And then they left together.

I don't believe it! thought Lillian. Surely Izzy was made of firmer stuff than that! It seemed she couldn't be sure of anyone anymore. Everyone seemed fickle and unknowable.

She didn't want to bump into them, and so she waited a few moments before leaving. Perhaps she was jumping to conclusions. It could be a simple lunch meeting, after all, to discuss the new changes in the office. But the way Rockwell had almost embraced Izzy as he helped her on with her coat told another story.

Lillian walked to the elevator and pressed the button. What was Izzy thinking? And with poor Red lying wounded! And with Rockwell, of all people. Famous for making passes at the new girls, with no regard whether they had husbands or beaus fighting overseas.

She suddenly remembered that she had left her sketchbook sitting out, where prying eyes might see it. She returned to the office and walked back to the switchboard to retrieve it. Then she stopped in her tracks: there was Mr. Weeble with her sketchbook in his hands, leafing through the pages!

Weeble heard her gasp, and whipped around, guilt all over his face.

"Mr. Weeble!" cried Lillian. She snatched the sketchbook from him. "That's private property!" She gave him a one-second chance to explain himself, but he just blinked and never said a word. Lillian stuffed the sketchbook into her bag and left in a huff. Surely the war can't be blamed for everything, she thought.

Over lunch at the diner, Lillian browsed through her sketches to see if there was anything incriminating that Weeble could report to Mr. Rockwell. She soon realized that none of her drawings had anything to do with work, except for that one old drawing of Mr. Weeble as a lizard. Nothing at her job inspired or moved her. Rather, the sketches depicted street vendors, architectural details, sunlight shooting through clouds, fanciful landscapes.

She ate quickly and used the remainder of her lunch break to try to walk off her growing bewilderment with everything. Charles was distancing himself from her. Izzy had brushed her aside. She took a deep breath. You're on your own, she told herself; you've been through hard times before. Toughen up, as Izzy said, and deal with it. Well, she thought, part of toughening up would be to confront Izzy. That would be a good place to start.

But Izzy purposely avoided her for the rest of the day. Every time Lillian passed her, Izzy pretended to be busy with something. Lillian's temper was rising; she would not be put off. She was determined to speak with Izzy, whatever the result.

Lillian caught up with her after work, had to practically run after Izzy as she was leaving the building.

"Izzy! Wait up. I'll walk with you to the bus stop."

Izzy waited for her to catch up, but didn't say anything.

"Izzy, what's going on? I know something is bothering you. You haven't –"

"I'm fine."

Lillian felt a flush of anger at being brushed off; she quickened her pace to keep up.

"Izzy, you had lunch with Mr. Rockwell? Do you really think that was a good idea?"

"Yes, I had lunch with him, and I'm going to have dinner with him on Friday."

Lillian stopped. "You can't be serious! You know what kind of man he is. This goes beyond business."

"Look, Lilly. He's helped me, promoted me, given me a chance. That's more than anyone else has done." She continued walking, thrusting her hands into her pockets.

Lillian caught up and took her arm, forcing Izzy to face her. "What about Red? How can you do this while he lies wounded?"

"Red can take care of himself." Izzy kept walking, leaving Lillian stunned by her words.

"Izzy! How can you talk like that?" Lillian cried, once again hurrying to catch up with her. "Is this simply because he postponed the wedding? Maybe he was right about that," she said, hearing Charles's argument come out of her mouth.

Izzy spun around. "Is that what you've been telling yourself? Let me tell you something. When a man says no to marriage, it means only one thing. He's changed his mind about you. It's as simple as that. See you around, Lilly."

The verbal punch caused Lillian to stand stuck to the ground. Those were cruel words. Directed at her. And Charles. Were they true? Could everyone see it but her? Maybe Charles didn't want to hurt her. Maybe he was hoping she would read between the lines, so he wouldn't have to spell it out for her.

The fissure between her and Charles cracked wider; his distance suddenly made sense to her.

She began to walk quickly, not heeding where she was going. You really are on your own, she thought again, this time fully believing it.

The city swarmed around her, car horns blaring, sirens shrieking, street vendors shouting. Lillian walked down the busy avenue, the crowds jostling her in an abrasive, jarring manner. She wanted to be far away from the troubled and troublesome world. She glanced up at the sky – it was too late to go to the park, her usual refuge after a trying day.

She crossed over to Fifth Avenue and walked a few blocks until she came to Saint Patrick's Cathedral. She often ducked into chapels and churches when she wanted to be alone, or was in need of an infusion of beauty and tranquility.

As she neared the cathedral, she saw sandbags and barricades – air raid preparations. What was wrong with the world? she wondered, as she climbed the steps to the cathedral.

She pulled open the heavy bronze door and stepped inside, entering into another world.

All her senses shifted.

There was an immediate hush. The traffic from outside became muffled and distant. She listened and heard only small sounds from inside: the clicking of heels along the aisles, a few muted murmurs and whispering. A lingering scent of incense filled the cool, still air, as if years and years of the perfumed smoke had permeated the stone.

She stood a moment at the back of the cathedral, and raised her eyes to the stained glass windows, dark in the fading day, and to the pillars that rose up, their tops branching out into delicately ribbed supports that formed star patterns in the vaulted ceiling. Lantern-like chandeliers hung high above the pews, adding to the diffused light that filled the cathedral, except for where a sculpture, a painting, or an altar was illuminated. Down the nave, at the opposite end, the high altar and pulpit appeared tiny, almost doll-sized.

It was an immense space, yet intimate, as if the cathedral itself formed protective hands fingertipped together in prayer. Immense, but studded with human-scale details: the fonts of holy water, the candles flickering along the periphery in the various altars, the clusters of white poinsettias placed near the altar, the carved wooden doors of the confessionals. A space designed for two different scales, two different concepts: one small and human, the other vast and invisible; one measured in hours and days, the other existing beyond clock time, suggestive of infinity.

Lillian walked up the side aisle, stopping before the small altars of the various saints who nestled in the alcoves and appeared comfortable with their aloneness, and with the people who kneeled before them, desirous of their blessing.

She paused before the altar of Saint Louis, drawn by the interplay of colors in the tiles and mosaics – luminous white, green, gold. She lifted one of the wooden sticks into a candle flame, and with its fire, lit a votive candle set in ruby glass. The flame caught and grew, and another tiny light was added to the shrine. The corners of her lips lifted as she realized she had moved from observer to participant; some exchange had taken place. Her vague longing or dim asking had been answered, or perhaps countered, with a flickering flame.

She walked down the opposite aisle, admiring the shrines with their delicate details: the purity of carved white marble; the mosaics depicting vines of green and rose, others forming a backdrop of glittering gold; the richness of the colored glass holding the votive candles – rich umber, deep forest green, ruby, midnight blue – all quickened by the tiny flames illuminating the glass. Such purity and beauty and infinity in a simple point of light – the deep hues of the glass not revealed until the candle was lit within. Like the stained glass windows, she thought, lifting her eyes to observe them. Now in the dusk, the windows consisted of dark shapes and black leaden lines, their meaning invisible – until the sun would again shine through them. Then the windows would burst into being, animated with figures, stories, symbols, colors – the etherealness of light made visible.

Serenity surrounded Lillian and changed her inner landscape. The jagged worries and complaints lost their edges, and were smoothed into gentleness. Here was beauty. Solace. Meaning. Human longing and yearning, creating a space of intimate grandeur.

She slid into a pew and looked around her. It seemed there were more people in the cathedral, no doubt because of the war. She observed the kneeling figures, the heads bent in prayer. A low murmur came from an old woman in front of her, words of prayer, her old gnarled hands working a black-beaded rosary. Such devotion, such belief, quietly expressed with eyes closed and hands folded.

Lillian had come in feeling pulled in all directions by tension, fear, anger, in doubt of her place in the world. She brought herself back down to this hour, in this place, and tried to examine the source of her earlier inner turmoil. Calmer now, she rested her eyes on the back of the pew in front of her, and there lined up her jumble of concerns: a world at war and the effect it seemed to have on everyone; Izzy's harshness; the petty frustration with her job and the feeling of wasting her time. And the overarching ache, that Charles had perhaps changed his mind about her.

Izzy's right, Lillian thought. If Charles doesn't want to marry me, there's nothing I can do, and I won't press him. That's not something that can be forced. All I can do is keep trying to live in a manner that is true and right for me. Protect my children, make their world as safe and loving as possible. Try to do some good. Try to be at peace with the world. Try to connect to – she looked around, trying to find a word to describe this space – this timeless beauty. There was something bigger than the day to day, more powerful and more beneficent than what she might find on the street, at work, in people. This connection is what has been missing, she thought. Her connection to old, beautiful things, to the expressions of the human heart at work, attempting to create something of meaning and beauty.

In the alcove to her left, tiny flames glittered in the rows of ruby-glass votive candles. She imagined tiny whispers of warm air rising from them, rising up to the stained glass windows, up to the Gothic arches. She discreetly took out her sketchbook, and made a quick drawing of the candles; their wisps of smoke, like little prayers or thoughts of love, turned into tiny angels – spiraling up, up into the cathedral air.

She would finish the drawing at home. She tucked the sketchbook into her purse, and quietly left, the soft clicking of her heels, her thoughts, her love, becoming part of the cathedral.

Lillian opened the heavy brass doors, and walked out into the cold of the night. She stood at the top of the steps, taking in the bustling world all around, and smiled at the exuberant, striving, pulsating swirl of humanity playing out in front of her.

She walked down the steps and turned up Fifth Avenue, thinking, there are a thousand ways to drink from the world.

# Chapter 10

Mrs. Murphy and Brendan met every night after work. Brendan traded his night shifts to days, and took her to dinner at his favorite pubs. She helped him with his Christmas shopping; he helped her with her Christmas baking. On the weekend they rode the ferry around the Statue of Liberty, and spent an entire afternoon window-shopping along Fifth Avenue, stopping to listen to the carolers. Mrs. Murphy had the curious sensation that her life had suddenly become three-dimensional. Time seemed to be popping out at odd angles; time she never thought she had available was now filled with lunchtime strolls, evening outings. Brendan even surprised her with tickets to the Christmas show with the Rockettes at Radio City Music Hall, and they finished the evening with a visit to the Christmas tree at Rockefeller Center. The corners of her life, the corners of her mind were filled with time with Brendan.

Once or twice, she told herself to slow things down, reminding herself that all good things must come to an end. But each time she intended to say *no* to one of his larks, he pulled her arm, saying, "Come on, Mary! There's life to be lived!" And she gladly gave in. He had always used that line on her, and it had always worked. She had been as hungry for life as he had been.

But surely they had changed, she kept telling herself. Surely, they would have their fill, and then go back to their old lives. If things didn't settle down soon, she would have to help it along. Explain that enough was enough. Push the friendship back to the status of cards at Christmas. Tea, once or twice a year, perhaps.

Those were her sincere intentions. But she couldn't stop herself. She felt like she was living again, and the feeling was intoxicating. When Brendan asked her to spend either Christmas Eve or Christmas Day with him and meet his daughter and family, she had simply changed the subject, and avoided the confrontation she knew was coming. Sooner or later it would have to end, but she didn't want to miss out on a single day with him until then.

And sure enough, that day did come. In a messy, quarrelsome manner that she had not foreseen.

One afternoon, they strolled through Central Park, wending their way along the paths, crossing over bridges, stopping to look at the ducks in the lake, the bare trees against the gray sky, a few clopping horse carriages. A light snow began to fall, but it didn't cause them to pick up their pace. If anything, they walked more slowly, arms linked tightly under the umbrella, reluctant to leave the quiet and beauty of the winter day. One by one, the lamplights came on, shining brightly along the path before them. Mrs. Murphy felt a small tug at her heart – the loveliness of the golden lamplights in the darkening day filled her with sadness. They seemed to her to mark the end – of life, of dreams, of her time with Brendan.

By the time they left the park, night was settling in, and they now felt the cold. They decided to warm up at their favorite pub, a cozy little place off Times Square, with live Irish music – fiddles and flutes, and sometimes simple impromptu singing.

They took a table by the window, and slowly the place filled up. Over dinner they talked and laughed, and when the music began to play, Brendan prevailed upon her to dance with him. Mrs. Murphy surprised herself that she still remembered how.

They sat back down, flushed with the dance. Mrs. Murphy fanned herself with the menu, while Brendan went to get them drinks.

What a time they had! She had forgotten that a day could be so full.

She observed Brendan as he stood at the bar and ordered another pint for himself and a ginger beer for her. He had the air of a young man, the way he leaned back against the bar, one foot resting on the brass foot rail, laughing with the bartender. He had a broad chest, a thick head of nearly white hair, an energetic way of moving. She had the surprising thought that it would be a lovely, comforting thing to rest her head on his chest. When he suddenly turned and smiled at her, she felt her heart leap.

Brendan came back with their drinks and sat down across from her. He then took her hand, and held it tightly.

They turned to listen to the singer who had stepped up to the little area that served as a stage. In a clear tenor voice he began to sing "The Rose of Tralee."

Mrs. Murphy couldn't remember the last time she had felt so full, so brimming over with love and passion for life, for the beauty of music, and the companionship of a kindly man.

Brendan squeezed her hand. "I feel like a young man, Mary. I – I haven't been this happy in a long time. We always were good together." He laughed, and except for his white beard, he looked like a young man again. "Sure, as I live and breathe, I feel that nothing has changed."

He took her other hand and leaned in towards her, his eyes twinkling with happiness. "And though I may feel young, I'm too old to be beating around the bush," he said, with a small nervous laugh. "I once gave you a locket, because I didn't have money for a ring. But I do now."

Brendan reached into his vest pocket, took out a blue velvet box, and set it in front of her. Then he opened the lid, turned it towards her, and clasped both her hands again.

"I still want you for my wife, Mary. For whatever time we have left. Let's live our lives together. Let's make up for lost time."

Mrs. Murphy looked away. The love and hope in his eyes nearly broke her heart. Before she answered, she took a good look all around her, memorizing every detail of the moment. Outside the window, people hurried by, tucked beneath their hats against the snow, and couples strolled by arm in arm under a shared umbrella. Inside, laughter and warmth filled the pub, and the soft strain of "The Rose of Tralee" ached with longing and regret. And across from her sat a lovely man with a warm, gentle heart. Here she was, she thought, for this brief, fleeting moment, thick in the charm of life.

She closed her eyes, and impressed the memory on her mind so that she would never forget it.

Then she opened her eyes, and once more became the practical and efficient Mrs. Murphy. It was her own fault, she told herself. She was like a child who willfully ignored the fact that daylight was fading and time for play would soon be over. And now here it was – the fall of night, an end to play and dreams. She took a deep breath and looked Brendan in the eye.

But she couldn't speak the words. She tried, but they just wouldn't come.

When she didn't answer, Brendan gently asked the question that had been plaguing him every time he tried to fill in the gaps in her life.

"Mary dear, I don't mean to pry, but you've – you've never once mentioned your husband. I know you've lost him, and sure, I don't want to be stirring up painful memories. But – was he not good to you, Mary? Is that it? I swear to you, I'll never give you cause for pain or sorrow. Not a moment. I only want to make you happy."

She gave a light groan, laden with despair.

Brendan believed he had hit upon the answer, the reason why she held back, why she avoided talking about her past. He began to grow angry that anyone would dare hurt his sweet Mary Margaret.

"Is that it? Was he a drunk? Did he not treat you right?"

The pain in her eyes as she turned away stoked his imagination and he envisioned the worst.

"Oh, I could kill the brute if he ever laid a hand on you." He sat back, riling himself up for a fight. He made a fist, as if winding up to throw a punch. "You should have told me years ago. I would have come and, by God, if that husband of yours so much as hurt a hair on your head, why, I would have –"

"Brendan!" She couldn't let him go on like this.

He froze, his fist still in the air, surprised at the force of her tone.

"There was no husband," she said quietly.

Brendan stared open-mouthed, waiting for her words to make sense. He squinted, attempting to understand what she was saying. "But – I thought – Do you mean to tell me you never married?"

"No. I never married."

He sat back in his chair, trying to puzzle out what she meant. Then his head snapped up.

"Are you saying –" He pulled on his beard, trying to be broadminded about things, trying to rearrange his idea of the saintly Mary Margaret. "Are you saying – you two lived together? And never married? Was he a married man, then? Is that it?"

"Brendan Sullivan!" said Mrs. Murphy. She sat up straight and gave her jacket a quick tug. "How dare you think such a thing?" She was grateful that his words had shifted her sorrow to indignation. It would make the rest easier. She gathered her coat around her shoulders and slipped her arms through the sleeves, and then began to pull on her gloves.

"Come. It's time we're off and away," she said. "It's getting late."

Brendan's world had just shifted, the earth was still wobbling beneath him.

"Now, hold on here, Mary. I'm not good at readin' between the lines." He leaned towards her, with pleading eyes. "Help me to understand what you're sayin' here –"

She responded as casually as if he had just asked her the time. "There was no one." She pulled smooth her gloves, and held her purse in front of her on the table. She held his eyes, and spoke with just a glimmer of regret. "There was you. And then there was no one."

Brendan waited for her to say more. Then he looked away, blinking in incomprehension. He squinted again, and cocked his head.

"But – but I understood you were to marry – that you intended to marry someone else." He became agitated now, as if learning that some life-long joke had been played on him, and he was just now catching on.

The accusatory tone in his voice spurred Mrs. Murphy to take the defensive. "I never said or implied such a thing." She put on her hat, and again held her position behind her purse.

Brendan scooted his chair back loudly, hands on his thighs. "But – when you broke off – it was because you – you had someone else –"

She waved his words away. "What nonsense you've always talked. I never said anything of the sort. Come, let's go."

"What are you sayin'?" his voice louder now, his brogue returning. "You led me to believe – I remember clearly –"

"I told you simply that I had changed my mind. That something prevented my marrying you. And not to make a fuss about it."

He shot to his feet, unable to believe what he was hearing.

"No, Mary Margaret Murphy! Don't you dare tell me those words! Not now! Not after all these years. You told me there was someone else," he said, pointing his finger at her. "That was the only reason, the only way I would ever have let you go. I remember like it was yesterday, you said there was someone else –"

Mrs. Murphy also stood and gripped the sides of the table, her voice raised.

"Don't you dare tell *me* what I said, Brendan Sullivan! I remember my words exactly: 'There's *something* that prevents me marrying you.' My exact words!"

"You said there's *someone* else!"

"'There's *something* else!'" She slapped her hand down on the table. "Those were my very words. By God, I should know – I practiced them enough times never to forget a single one of them!"

They stood leaning in towards each other, both of them gripping the sides of the table, anger and desperation in their eyes.

The tenor stopped singing. The talking and laughter around them ceased. All eyes were on the couple who just a few moments earlier had appeared to be a happily married couple still deeply in love. Everyone watched for who would break the tension-filled face-off – the man who looked remarkably like Santa Claus, or the woman who appeared his equal in passion and strength.

Then the woman's face crumpled, and she hastened from the pub, leaving behind her the large, barrel-chested man, still gripping the table.

Mrs. Murphy ran out and hailed a cab, ignoring the hot tears burning in her eyes – as she once more fled the presence of the only man she had ever loved. Once more leaving him alone, and without the truth.

Brendan stumbled back into his chair. Stunned. His whole life had just been flipped over. The long, quarrelsome years with Elizabeth. The anger that filled him over the years. And now – now to realize that he had been ousted by, jealous of, a phantom?

An idea? How many times had he imagined what the fellow might look like? What their lives together were like, while his was bitter. How many times did he take out the crushed rose from that evening? How many times did he cry tears into his pillow, trying to hate her, but unable to overcome his love? And now – now to hear that there was no one?

Then why? Why? He tried to imagine what else it could have been. And had to face the only answer he could come up with. That she had never loved him the way he loved her. Didn't want to share her life with him. It's as simple as that, he told himself. You old fool.

He took the tiny blue box in his large hand, closed the lid, and pocketed the evidence of his foolishness. He finished off his drink in one quick swig, and allowed himself another stunned moment of staring out at nothing.

One of the musicians began to play a merry tune on the fiddle, and slowly the foot tapping and head bobbing resumed, and conversations took up where they had left off. For the most part, people turned their eyes away from the man resembling Santa, who looked very much as if he might cry.

*

Mrs. Murphy had hurried home, paced around her apartment in an attempt to walk off her anger and distress, and had finally taken a hot bath. She was now trying to regain the composure and presence of mind that had always been her habit. She was shocked that she had behaved like a schoolgirl.

Calmer now, she forced herself to review her past. Forty years ago she had been a young girl, bursting with confidence and a mad passion for life. She had been proud of her trim figure, her mass of dark curls, proud that she had caught the eye of the man she had been so smitten by – a tall, handsome man who had just started rooming at the boarding house down the street. All the girls had been wild about him – but he had eyes for her alone.

There began the sweetest courtship, one that had wheels of its own that nothing could have stopped. Brendan was a determined young man, studying and working his way up from machinist to engineer. He was on his own, and lived life according to his belief: "There's life to be lived!" Those words had convinced her to run in the rain with him, to row on the river Charles, to walk the city from dawn to dusk, and to defy her parents' plea to wait until they were older to court. She had accepted Brendan's attentions, convinced her parents, and had never known such happiness. A year of life bursting at the seams, of plans for living life to the hilt, and of someday starting a family of their own.

They had spent nearly every evening together that summer. She attributed her growing fatigue to their escapades and larks, and to the fact that love had taken all her energy – and well worth the trade it was.

The night Brendan gave her the locket and asked her to marry him was the most magical night of her life, a pinnacle moment against which nothing else had ever come close. He had taken her to the little restaurant along the water. Had presented her with a heart-shaped locket, as good as an engagement ring.

They had then strolled in the warm summer breeze along the banks of the Charles, and sat on their bench where they often watched the lights twinkling on in the dusk. They had each picked a bright red rose from the bushes that grew alongside the bench, brought the roses to their lips, and handed them to each other.

And she had said, of course, she would marry him. And they had kissed the sweetest kiss, the promise of a closeness that would soon be theirs. She still blushed to remember her boldness, how that night, for the first time, she had let him place his hand under her blouse and cup his hand around her breast. And Brendan had spoken words of pure love and tenderness: "Sure, but I'm holding a bit of heaven in my hand," he had said. "A bit of heaven."

Mrs. Murphy stood before her mirror now, forty years later, and admitted that she had been a coward. The strong front of bravado and confidence that she had so easily worn all these years, fell away as she stood vulnerable in her robe, before her bedroom mirror. She had turned off the overhead light; the room was softly illuminated by the small lamp that stood next to her bedside. She had long ago traded the white shade for a pink shade, the rosy light being far more forgiving for nights such as this, when she reminded herself of why she had chosen the path in life that left her alone at age sixty – an office manager, instead of a wife; an aunt, instead of a mother.

She took a deep breath and slowly parted her robe, letting it fall around her shoulders. The locket that she had never taken off rested on her chest, above the two scars that had long ago replaced her breasts. They no longer shocked or repulsed her. She felt pity for them, as if they were two independent little beings she had cared for, protected all these years. She pulled her robe closed, climbed into bed, and turned off the lamp.

With her hand around the locket, she buried her face in her pillow, and allowed herself one last act of weakness, and then she would once again become the strong and cheerful Mrs. Murphy that everyone believed her to be. She allowed tears to pour forth, weeping for that younger self, for the pain she had caused her dear Brendan, for the youthful dreams that had come to naught. One last act of girlishness, before that old chapter was closed forever.

# Chapter 11

❦

On Saturday afternoon, Lillian glanced up from her ironing to see what the boys were arguing about. Tommy sat at the kitchen table, enjoying a piece of the chocolate raspberry cake and washing it down with a glass of milk. His baseball glove sat next to his plate, and in between bites he slipped it on and punched it a few times.

"I said, where is it?" asked Gabriel, looking around the counter, lifting covers, opening the bread drawer. He then realized that Tommy had eaten the last piece of cake.

"Hey! I was saving that for Tiny!" cried Gabriel.

Lillian lifted one of Tommy's shirts out of the laundry basket and sprinkled it with water. "Tommy! You were supposed to share that piece with Gabriel."

"I asked you if I could have it," said Tommy. "And you said *yes*."

"Well, I didn't know that was the piece Gabriel was saving. And I told you to share it with him." She began to press the shirt. "How about some cookies and milk, Gabriel?"

"You knew that was my piece," Gabriel said. "That wasn't very nice, Tommy."

"Here," said Tommy, cutting a piece of imaginary cake, and placing it on an imaginary plate. "I saved this piece just for Tiny. It's his favorite."

Lillian was afraid Gabriel might punch Tommy, or at the very least say something smart to him. But he simply took out a checked napkin and wrapped a few apples in it, added a bag of Annette's toffee, and then placed the bundle into his burlap bag of sticks. A snack for the ball game, she guessed, and breathed a sigh of relief.

Tommy put his dishes in the sink, and mussed Gabriel's hair. "Come on, Gabe. Let's go beat the Bulldogs. Don't forget your glove. We might need you to field."

The boys put on their coats and caps and headed for the door.

"Gabriel, do you really need to take that big bag with you?" asked Lillian.

"Just stuff for our game," answered Tommy, wanting to avoid any delays. "Don't worry, Mom. We'll be home before dark."

"Keep an eye on Gabriel," she called after them.

"Bye, Mom!" both boys hollered as they ran down the stairs.

Gabriel was upset with Tommy for eating the piece of cake, and remained silent on their way to the park.

Tommy playfully pulled down the brim of Gabriel's cap. "Aw, c'mon. Don't be sore. I'll buy you a piece of cake at the diner later."

They crossed over into the park and fell in with the other boys. The Bulldogs won the coin toss and batted first. Gabriel waited until the second inning when Tommy was at bat, and then he ducked away to take his bag of sticks to Tiny.

One block up, and three blocks over. Gabriel had only been to Tiny's building once before, but just outside on the steps, never inside. He recognized the building and walked up to the stoop. He stepped around the shards of glass on the sidewalk, and was careful not to wake the man who was propped up against the wall, sound asleep with an empty bottle in his hand.

Gabriel opened the front door, and climbed the dark flights of stairs. Tobacco smoke and cooking smells filled the air. On the second floor, a door stood open, and sounds of something sizzling and the banging of utensils mixed with other sounds in the building: a man and a woman yelling, a door opening and closing, a burst of laughter. When Gabriel reached the fourth floor he heard an angry baby crying; he could almost see the tiny fists shaking with each warbled wail.

Tiny had told him that he and his brother lived at the very top. Gabriel climbed the fifth flight, and saw that it was the last; it leaned at an odd angle, with a long rod braced against the wall opposite – to keep it from falling down, Gabriel supposed.

At the top floor, two doors were boarded over, so Gabriel knocked at the third door. No one answered. He knocked again. "It's me, Tiny. Gabriel! I brought your sticks."

The door cracked open and Tiny peeked out. He then opened the door to let Gabriel in. "I thought you were the police."

"The police?" asked Gabriel, glancing behind him before stepping inside.

"We owe rent. My brother lost his job when he got sick." Tiny closed the door, and slid a lock into place. "Mrs. Malden rents out the rooms and says we can stay until she finds another renter. She lives on the first floor. Her legs are bad."

"Oh." Gabriel stood near the door, blinking as his eyes adjusted to the gloom.

"I carry coal for her from the cellar, run errands, and chase her cat down when it runs away," continued Tiny. "She says I'm working out the rent.

But when the landlord comes he says we're squatters, and is going to call the police on us."

Gabriel turned a troubled face to Tiny.

"Don't worry. He only comes at the beginning of the month, so we're safe for now. Come on in."

Tiny walked over to a mattress that was set against the wall, next to a tiny wood burning stove and an up-side-down crate that served as a table – the only furniture in the place.

"This is my brother." Tiny knelt down next to the mattress. "Hey, Marcel, this is my friend, Gabriel, that I told you about. He brought us some firewood."

Gabriel looked down on a pitifully thin man, or boy. As with Tiny, Gabriel couldn't tell for sure which one he was. The blanket was pulled up to Marcel's chin, and on top of the blanket lay an old black overcoat, tucked around him like an empty embrace. Dark shadows surrounded his eyes, and his breathing was slow and laborious. A tiny ripple seemed to take place deep in his chest after each breath, followed by a long pause before another intake of breath. It reminded Gabriel of the little warble at the end of the long, drawn-out cries of the angry baby; he wished their mothers could come and make them better.

"Hi, Marcel," Gabriel said softly, kneeling down beside the bed. "I brought you guys something. Sticks, and some food. I was going to bring you a piece of cake, but Tommy ate it." He reached into his bag and pulled out the small bundle of apples and the bag of toffee, and placed them on the crate, next to some dried autumn leaves that Tiny must have gathered – faded yellow, orange, and curled up red. "Some apples from my aunt's orchard."

Marcel shifted slightly under the covers, as if he wanted to say or do something, but gave it up.

"Gee, thanks, Gabriel," said Tiny.

Gabriel shivered in the chill air. But Tiny was now stuffing the stove with sticks, and soon a little warmth poured over them in the cramped attic room.

"I was just reading to brother." He held up a tattered book. "*The Count of Monte Cristo*. Have you read it?"

"No," said Gabriel, running his finger over the words on the blue book.

"You gotta get it. It's great. Right, brother?"

Marcel gave the smallest of nods.

"Okay," said Gabriel. "My mom will get it at the library. She reads to me. Tommy used to, but he doesn't anymore." Gabriel turned to Marcel. "Tommy's my brother. He's older than me. Just like you and Tiny."

Marcel tried to smile, then he closed his eyes and remained still.

Tiny untied the napkin and uncovered the treasures within. "Look at these, Marcel!" One by one, he polished the four red and green apples on his threadbare pants, and then arranged them on top of the crate, among the dried leaves. He cocked his head at the display of color in the otherwise gray room, and nodded in satisfaction.

Then he took the bag that held the toffee, and opened it. He almost choked in surprise.

"I don't believe it!" He lifted a small piece and waved it under his nose, closing his eyes in delight as he inhaled the scent. Then he broke off a chunk, put it in his mouth, and released an audible sigh. He broke off another piece.

"You're not going to believe what Gabriel brought us." He slid a piece into his brother's mouth and waited for his response.

Marcel opened his eyes and blinked at the taste, and then turned to Tiny and smiled.

Gabriel saw that Marcel's chest rose and fell more smoothly now, and that his eyes were brighter. Gabriel leaned over to Tiny and whispered, "I think the toffee is helping him."

"It sure is," answered Tiny. "Remember that, Marcel?" Tiny leaned back on an elbow and smiled. "Just like Christmas at the orphanage, right brother? Sister Rosetta and her Christmas toffee. Every year."

Tiny crunched on the toffee. "It's best to let it melt – it lasts longer that way. But sometimes I just can't wait." Tiny handed the bag to Gabriel.

Gabriel took a small piece and tried to let it melt.

"Those were good times," said Tiny. "Christmas Eve to the Epiphany. No better times than that." He and Marcel exchanged glances, and both laughed at the unspoken thought between them.

"We had a tradition of our own at the orphanage," Tiny explained. "Marcel would tell me a Christmas story about Mom and Pop – about the presents they gave us, the surprise visit from Father Christmas, some of the special dishes Mom cooked. Then we'd save our toffee to eat at the exact same time. We were in different dormitories because of our age, but they had lights-out at the same time. So we'd both go to sleep with that sweet, buttery taste in our mouths, dreaming of spicy kitchens, and Mom and Pop, and –"

Marcel said something that Gabriel couldn't make out.

Tiny laughed. "That's right. And beaches."

Marcel added a few more words, in between raspy breaths.

Tiny smiled. "Yep. That's right. We're going back there. Soon as brother gets better."

Tiny turned to Gabriel. "That's where we used to live. A long time ago. I don't remember it, but brother does. It was a warm place, by the ocean. Pop was a fisherman, right?" he nodded at his brother. "When he died, Mom brought us up here. She was sick. She used to have family here but she couldn't find them. That's how we ended up at the orphanage. She had to go to the hospital but she never came out. So we're going back. Where it's warm. It'll be good for brother's chest."

Tiny paused to pass some more toffee all around. "Father Dwyer has been looking for some of our family for us. He's the one who found us this place. He's been asking brother all about where we used to live, any names of relatives he remembers, writing to different dioceses in Florida and Louisiana. He found some Demains down in New Orleans. Says one of them is our uncle. Maybe we'll go there and look around."

Tiny's brother said something, then coughed with the effort, and closed his eyes.

"What did he say?" asked Gabriel.

"He said I have to go even if he can't." Tiny gently placed his hand under his brother's neck, and lifted his head while he gave him a sip of water from a tin cup.

"Marcel said when Mom was sick she told him that dying was just like changing your clothes. Sometimes your clothes just plain wear out and it gets time to change them. She said not to worry. That we would all be together again. No doubt about it. And she said whenever we wanted to talk to her, she would hear us."

Marcel struggled to say, "Tell Gabriel – about the Christmas tree," and for a brief moment Marcel was present, engaged in the conversation as he anticipated the description.

Tiny wriggled in excitement as he relived the memory, getting up on his knees to better tell the story. "Every Christmas at the orphanage, they put up a tree that reached to the ceiling of the assembly room. All week the nuns decorated it, but they kept the room locked so we couldn't see. Then a couple of days before Christmas –" Tiny slowly spread his arms wide. "They opened the doors, and there it was!"

Once again, Tiny was rapt with awe, his eyes traveling up limb to limb of the tall tree. "A huge Christmas tree, with shiny ornaments and red ribbons – and an angel on top. And streamers all around the room. We always knew it was going to be there, but it was always a surprise."

He sat back down on his heels, and was silent for a few moments. "Then on Christmas Eve we'd sing carols around the tree, and go to bed knowing that the next morning, at each of our seats in the dining hall, there would be presents. Wrapped up in Christmas paper, just for us." Tiny and his brother exchanged glances, and Marcel pointed to the book.

"Yep," said Tiny, handing the book to his brother. "This was one of brother's gifts the last year we were there.

Marcel rested both hands over the book, and fixed his eyes on Tiny.

"Those nuns, Gabriel. It was like having thirty moms. Sure, some of them were strict." He raised his eyebrows at his brother. "Sister Sebastian? Man, oh man. But she was fair. And she read to us every Friday afternoon. She knew of some good books: *On the Run, Huckleberry Finn, Corporal Downing Takes the Trail, Connie Morgan in Alaska* – that was a great one. Most of the books were for boys."

Tiny laughed at a memory that came to him. "One time, some of the boys goofed off, and Sister Sebastian announced that just for that, she was going to read *Heidi* – a girls' book! We all moaned and groaned. But then we liked it so much, we asked her to read it a second time. Yep, that was a really great story."

Tiny smiled, as if he were right back in the schoolroom, hands folded on his desk, once again seeing Heidi and her grandfather, and Peter and his goats, his blind grandmother and...

"Did you stay at the orphanage all the time?" asked Gabriel.

"Sure," said Tiny, returning from the Alps. "Where else would we go? A lot of kids were half-orphans and some of them went home over the summer, but most were like us. No parents. But summers were all right."

He looked to his brother for confirmation, and nodded. "There was a huge playground, with a merry-go-round that held about twenty kids. We'd run and get that thing spinning, and then all jump on. We'd go so fast, our caps would fly off. And some kids roller skated in the courtyard and down the driveway. I only had one skate, but I got pretty good at it."

"Where was the other skate?" asked Gabriel.

Tiny shrugged, as if the small detail didn't matter. He clasped his hands around his knees and rocked, pushing off with his toes, thinking about the good ole days.

He tipped his head to his brother. "We were lucky. Most of the kids were alone. But we always had each other. Ever since I was born I had my brother." Tiny's voice quivered a little, and he reached inside the bag for another piece of toffee, and gave it a firm crunch.

"This tastes *exactly* like Sister Rosetta's. It's like you brought us our old Christmas back. Thanks, Gabriel."

Gabriel watched Marcel, who remained motionless, and then looked back at Tiny. With a worried expression, Gabriel leaned in towards Marcel, waiting for him to move or cough or breathe or do something. But he just lay there with eyes closed, utterly still. Gabriel turned to Tiny. "Did he change his clothes?" he whispered.

Tiny caressed his brother's hand. "No. He's just sleeping."

Gabriel watched them for a few moments. "Will you still talk to me, Tiny, when you go to the warm place?"

"Course, I will." Tiny stretched out and rested his head on the mattress, and crossed one foot over his knee. He put his hands behind his head, and squinted across to the tiny single window, seeing beyond the streaky glass. "I might collect shells down there. Or help out with the fishing boats. Or I might just sit on the beach and eat coconuts."

Marcel began to cough and Tiny helped him to raise his head a little. Then Marcel lay back down on the pillow and closed his eyes. Tiny tucked the blanket back under his chin, and Marcel fell into sleep again.

Tiny leaned over to the crate and picked up a box of matches. He struck a match and lit a short candle stub in the darkening gloom. "There we go," he said cheerfully.

Gabriel looked over at the dark and dusty window. "Well, I guess I gotta go. My mom gets worried when it starts to get dark. She's kind of afraid of the dark."

"Okay. Thanks for the sticks," said Tiny, walking him to the door. "And the toffee. That made brother real happy."

Tiny's brow suddenly knitted in worry, and he looked quickly around the room. "Hold on Gabriel." He ran to the bed, and from underneath the mattress he pulled out his prized treasures, two books by Father Finn: *Sunshine and Freckles*, and *Tom Playfair*. He looked at the covers, and then handed the newer looking one to Gabriel.

"A gift from me and Marcel. *Tom Playfair* – you'll like it. About a boy who gets sent away to a boarding school. One of my Christmas presents at the orphanage."

"Gee, thanks!" Gabriel put the book inside his jacket. "So long, Tiny. Say bye to Marcel for me."

Tiny walked Gabriel to the door, and once again poked his head out into the hall. "The coast is clear. See you around, Gabriel."

Gabriel walked in near darkness down the leaning stairs. The man and woman were still arguing, but the baby must have fallen asleep.

Gabriel left the building, stepping over the man who was now stretched out on the bottom step. Then he ran all the way back to the park.

The game had run into extra innings. The score was locked in a tie, with one out. Gabriel saw that Tommy was up to bat.

"Come on, Tommy!" he yelled along with the other boys. "Slug it!"

Tommy swung once, almost spinning in a complete circle, but missed the ball. He swung at the second pitch, and Gabriel cheered when Tommy got a hit. The ball arced high up, and then landed smack in the shortstop's glove. Tommy kicked at the dirt, and ran back. Two outs.

Tommy walked over to Gabriel, remembering him all of a sudden.

"Where were you?"

Gabriel pointed to where he had crossed into the park. "Over there."

But Tommy was biting his nails, focused on the next batter. Mickey walked up to the plate, bent his knees, and planted his feet. He connected with the ball on the first pitch, sending it straight down the center, and then ran like lightning. Spider, who was standing just behind second base, missed the ball and had to chase it down, and wrestled it away from the center fielder. Then he threw it wide to the short stop, enabling Mickey to make it all the way home. Tommy and the Redbirds cheered at their win, and tossed their caps high into the air.

Butch threw his glove down and shook his head at Spider, but most of his team shook hands with the Redbirds and were already talking about starting up again in the spring. Spider was a poor sport and sulked.

"Cheer up, Spider! You have all winter to practice," taunted Tommy.

"I had something in my eye, ya sap!" said Spider. "Anyway, you're no great shakes. Always hitting pop-ups."

Tommy waved his words away, and slapped Mickey on the back.

"We're number one!" the Redbirds began to chant.

By now it was getting dark and Tommy and Gabriel quickly gathered their things. "So long!" they cried out to the band of boys.

"Did you see the double I hit in the fifth?" asked Tommy. "And the fly ball I caught?"

Gabriel smiled, happy that Tommy's team won the game.

"And I only struck out twice."

"Wow! You're going to be the best player on the whole team."

"Nah," said Tommy. "Mickey's the best. Did you see that ball he slammed? Right down the middle."

Lillian had been waiting for Tommy and Gabriel to return, but when it started to get dark she decided to go to the park to check up on them.

As Tommy and Gabriel were leaving the park, they saw her on the other side of the street, ready to cross over to the park.

"Uh oh," said Tommy. "I think we're in trouble."

They ran over to her and Tommy started explaining quickly, not giving her a chance to scold him. "Sorry, Mom, but it was a tie game, and we couldn't stop. We had to go into extra innings, and then Mickey slugged it, and Spider missed the ball, and we won! And you should have seen the double I hit."

Lillian put an arm around both boys as Tommy recounted the highlights of the game, re-enacting the heroics of his team.

"Come on," said Lillian. "We have to stop at Mancetti's on our way home." She looked down at Gabriel, who seemed unusually quiet.

"Did you have fun, Gabriel?"

He nodded. "Mommy, will you get me *The Count of Monte Cristo* from the library?"

"*The Count of Monte Cristo*? Where did you hear about that? It's a thick novel."

"That's okay. Tommy will read it to me, won't you, Tommy?"

"Not if it's long."

"Please? It'll be fun."

"Read it yourself," said Tommy.

Lillian gave Tommy a look of disapproval. "We'll go to the library next week and get some books to read over your Christmas break."

"Okay," said Gabriel. "Mommy, if I have to be in the orphanage, will you still talk to me?"

Lillian stopped and bent down next to him. "Gabriel! You won't ever have to go to an orphanage. But no matter where I am, I will always talk to you."

Gabriel turned to Tommy. "Will you, Tommy?"

"Probably not."

"Tommy!" cried Lillian. "Why have you grown so rude all of a sudden? I think you spend too much time with some of those boys. I don't like the things you've been picking up from them."

"Mom, I'm getting tired of him always talking about imaginary people and orphanages. He didn't learn that from the guys. He just makes things up in his head."

"No, I don't," said Gabriel.

Lillian put an arm around Gabriel's shoulder. "Maybe we can get a new coloring book at Mancetti's. Would you like that, Gabriel?"

He bobbed his head up and down.

Inside Mancetti's, she let Tommy pick out a new comic book and Gabriel a coloring book. Then they walked to the back meat counter and waited, while Mrs. Wilson finished up with her order.

"Evening, Mrs. Hapsey. Hello, boys. Mr. Mancetti was just telling me that his store has been vandalized lately by a gang of boys. Graffiti – and he caught them throwing an egg earlier."

Lillian saw that Mancetti was frowning at Tommy from under his brows as he wrapped up the order for Mrs. Wilson. She turned to Tommy. "Do you know anything about that, Tommy?"

"No." When he saw that his mom and Mancetti and Mrs. Wilson were all looking at him, he threw his hands up. "Mom, I was playing ball. You saw me."

"He was at the park all afternoon. I don't think he knows anything," she said to Mancetti.

Mrs. Wilson took her packages of lunch meat and tossed them into her basket. "I'm sure it's those boys from the other side of Broadway who've been hanging about." She patted Tommy on his head as she passed.

Lillian took the list from her handbag. "I'll have a quarter pound of bologna and ten slices of cheddar." As Mancetti sliced and wrapped her order, she read over her list. Then she suddenly remembered what Gabriel had said. "Mr. Mancetti, is there a little boy who does errands for you?"

Tommy groaned and looked up at the ceiling, shaking his head.

"We've never needed any help," said Mancetti. "We've always managed ourselves."

Lillian wondered why he was so annoyed by her question. He was always grumpy, but he had grown even more so lately. She assumed that some customers had either stopped coming to the store, or were giving him a hard time, now that Italy was an enemy.

When they walked to the checkout counter, Tommy rolled his eyes. "Jeez, Mom, you're starting to sound like Gabriel."

"I just wanted to make sure. You never know."

"Mom," said Tommy, "it's like Taffy, the talking teddy bear. When Gabriel was five – don't you remember?

"Tiny's not a teddy bear," said Gabriel. "He's a real person."

"Whatever you say, Gabriel," said Tommy.

On the way home, Lillian looked down at her boys. Sometimes they were the best of friends. Other times, Tommy pushed Gabriel away, wanting his independence. Tommy was growing up, and rebelling in little ways. But Gabriel. His comment about being an orphan concerned her.

They passed Mickey and some of the Redbirds sitting on Mickey's stoop. "We're the champs!" they hollered to Tommy.

Lillian smiled to see both Tommy and Gabriel raise their hands in triumph and cheer back. Gabriel was often a puzzle to her. Sometimes she worried that he was overly sensitive; and yet he always surprised her by his unshakable resilience.

# Chapter 12

෴

Lillian stayed up late on Sunday, finishing another watch cap. Earlier in the week she had bought some black yarn, and had already knitted several caps. She now thought she would try to knit a sweater. As she cast on the stitches, she became aware of a sense of unease, some discontent that hadn't quite risen to the surface.

Was it concern about Gabriel? She thought of the matinee she and Charles had taken the boys to that afternoon. Gabriel had enjoyed *Dumbo*. In the beginning of the movie, Gabriel threw her a worried look when Dumbo's mother was taken away and locked inside a cage, reminding her of his comments about the orphanage. But other than that, Gabriel had loved the movie, and he clapped his hands when Dumbo discovered that his big ears were a good thing, enabling him to fly. Gabriel had leaned over to her and whispered, "He's like Rudolph, Mommy. Nobody liked him at first, either."

No, she thought. It wasn't Gabriel that was bothering her. He was a happy little boy. And Tommy was fine. It was something else.

Charles? She put her knitting down, and looked into the empty fireplace. She had come to accept his decision. And would wait. Wait for him to change his mind, wait for the war to be over. Wait.

Izzy. It was Izzy. Her words had swelled inside like festering barbs. Because every word was true, Lillian had to admit. She did need to toughen up. About everything. She couldn't control Charles or his actions, but she could control her own. If she didn't like her job at the switchboard, it was up to her to do something about it. If she wanted to move ahead with her work as an artist, it was in her own hands.

She would start again. And again and again. However long it took. She would take her portfolio with her to work, and use her lunch hour to take it around. The worst anyone could say was *no*. She would use all those rejections to toughen herself up. At least she would get something out of it that way.

As she worked on the sweater, she had the idea that a drawing related to the war would be her strongest calling card. Different themes and images ran through her mind: a soldier kissing his girl goodbye at a train station; Uncle Sam with bushy eyebrows and a tri-color top hat; a simple poster encouraging people to buy War Bonds; young men lined up outside a recruiting station. Then an image appeared in her mind, in full color and detail: A Victory Garden. She would draw a Victory Garden. The newspapers were already suggesting them, and everyone was sure to plant one in the spring. It would be a way of offsetting the dreadfulness of war – growing your own vegetables, connecting with the earth, taking care of something, and then harvesting the produce for the colder months ahead.

She put her knitting away, and took out her sketch pad. Using her colored pencils, she began a drawing based on her childhood home: a large garden was planted at the back of a two-story house, along with a strawberry patch and a grape arbor. She sketched a broad-shouldered father picking tomatoes and cucumbers that his two sons then collected into pails; the mother wore a floral apron and held a basket of bright green beans and red peppers. Lillian studied the drawing and sighed; she had drawn an idealized version of herself, the boys, and Charles. As a family.

It was well past midnight when she finished the drawing, but she felt energized, hopeful, determined. She had one more day at work before the holiday began. She would use her lunch hour to take her portfolio to a few design firms.

\*

The next morning Lillian dressed in her best gray suit and pearls. When she arrived at work, she almost bumped against Mr. Weeble with her portfolio. She had hoped to get to her desk without being noticed by him. For a moment, she thought he was going to say something, but rather than give him a chance to chastise her, she simply ignored him and went directly to the switchboard room.

The morning flew by as she sat at the switchboard and answered the lights, planning where she would go on her lunch hour, what she would say.

She dashed out at noon and managed to stop by three design offices over her break. She asserted herself when they told her to wait, saying that she only had fifteen minutes to present her work, before her next appointment. The simple truth had worked, and each place had agreed to take a brief look at her portfolio. The first one was not interested, the next told her to check back in a month, but the last one loved the Victory Garden and wanted to see more war-related drawings.

All in all, she was pleased with the results. In less than twenty-four hours, she had taken her career in a forward direction, and had made some progress. She wished she could share the news with Izzy. But every time she tried to approach her, Izzy turned her head, busy with something. Lillian worried that Izzy appeared strained, as if she hadn't slept, and had tried to cover the evidence with a thick layer of powder.

When Lillian gathered her things at the end of day, she realized that her portfolio was missing. She searched again and again, but it was nowhere in the switchboard room. In a panic, she feared that she had left it at the last design firm, or possibly on the bus. Her heart sank. It would be impossible to recreate all the drawings. She was ready to burst into tears of frustration.

But then she remembered that she had accidentally bumped someone in the elevator with her portfolio on her return to the office. It must be here, she thought. Perhaps someone moved it when she went to the ladies' room.

She suddenly stood up with her hands on her hips. Weeble! In a flash, Lillian knew he was behind it. She marched to his desk, ready to have it out with him. He was probably trying to get her fired, convince Rockwell that she was sketching on their time.

A few employees were still busy at their desks, but most had already left for the day. Lillian stepped up to the platform where Weeble's desk stood – and gasped. There was her open portfolio on his desk – empty! She feared the worst. She briefly imagined a demonic Mr. Weeble feeding the drawings into a fire, or cutting them up with a pair of scissors as he chuckled to himself.

She glanced over at Rockwell's office. Through the partially closed door she saw the back of Weeble, talking to Mr. Rockwell who was sitting at his desk, cigar in hand.

She walked up to Rockwell's office and pushed the door open. Weeble froze, with his mouth open, alarmed at having been caught. Rockwell lightly chuckled.

"Mrs. Hapsey," began Weeble. "Forgive me for taking your portfolio, but –"

"You're no better than a common thief!" Lillian began to gather up her drawings, relieved that they hadn't been hurt, though she was still throbbing with indignation. "Always snooping, spying on my every move! First my sketchbook. Now this? Really, Mr. Weeble!"

"Mrs. Hapsey –" began Rockwell, leaning back in his chair.

"And you!" she said, turning on Rockwell, still angry at him on behalf of poor Red. "Making passes at the girls whose soldiers are off fighting. You should be ashamed of yourself! Both of you!" She took her drawings and strode out of the room.

Lillian was still shaking when she went to the open portfolio on Weeble's desk and began placing her drawings inside. Slowly, she began to calm down as she stacked them one by one, and then closed her portfolio. Only now did she wonder if she had perhaps overreacted. No harm was done, after all. Her drawings were intact.

She heard a raucous laugh coming from Rockwell. "Are you sure you can handle such a firecat in your department, Weeble?" He laughed again. "Get her back in here."

Weeble walked up to his desk as Lillian was tying up her portfolio. She faced him, waiting for an explanation. His spectacles glinted as he looked everywhere but directly at her. "Mrs. Hapsey, I'm sorry I didn't ask for your permission, but I was afraid you would –"

He looked up and, on seeing her still furious, he lost his nerve. "Mr. Rockwell wishes to see you," he said, reverting to his usual stiff manner. He pivoted on his heel, and returned to Rockwell's office, planting himself just outside.

"I'm sure he does!" She mustered up what courage and dignity she could find, and with her portfolio under her arm, she walked back into Mr. Rockwell's office.

"Have a seat," said Rockwell. "Weeble! Get in here and finish what you started!"

Lillian remained standing and continued to glare at Weeble when he came in. Rockwell folded his hands behind his head and leaned back in his chair, as if about to enjoy a bit of entertainment.

"These drawings mean a great deal to me," said Lillian. "It took me years to put this collection together, and I don't appreciate anyone taking liberties with them, treating them as if they –"

Rockwell held up a hand for her to stop, and then cocked his head to the side. "It's clear, Mrs. Hapsey, that you're wasting your talent at the switchboard."

"I didn't mean to imply that, I only meant –"

"Weeble here has been singing your praises for months. Said you'd be more valuable in the Art Department."

Lillian opened her mouth and stared hard at Rockwell, not understanding what he was getting at. What exactly was he saying? Was she being fired?

"And after seeing your portfolio, I'm inclined to agree with him. So, if you can step off your high horse for a moment, I'd like to offer you a position as an illustrator."

Lillian still didn't speak. She looked from Rockwell, to Weeble, and back to Rockwell.

"Don't let it go to your head. Many of the men will be leaving soon. If you're ambitious, I suggest you take the job. Those getting in on the ground floor will have the greater chance for advancement." He waited for her to say something. "Well, are you interested or not? Speak up!"

"Yes." Lillian swallowed. "Yes, I am. Of course! That's exactly what – Thank you. Thank you, Mr. Rockwell. I'm sorry I –"

Rockwell put his hand up again. "No apologies needed. We need talent and you got it." He thumped his thick finger on the drawing of the Victory Garden. "Get this ready for February production, Weeble." He turned to Lillian, pointing to the wife in the drawing. "Make her a blonde, and make the husband younger. Make one of the kids a girl, with pigtails."

"Yes, sir," said Lillian.

"Get her set up, starting Monday," he said to Weeble. His phone began to ring and he answered it, and then waved them away, ending the conversation. "And find another girl for the switchboard!" he hollered, as Weeble and Lillian left the office.

Weeble closed the door after him and stood with his hands behind his back, looking rather pleased with himself.

Lillian realized that she had never seen him smile before. "Mr. Weeble. I don't know what to say. I thought you were working against me all this time. I thought you disliked my drawings."

"Only my likeness as a lizard – and even that was very good," he joked, rocking on his heels and straightening his spectacles. "I know what it's like to have a passion for something other than all this," he said, waving his hand over the office.

Lillian waited for him to explain himself. "You – you have another interest?"

"Radio," he beamed. "I've been tinkering with radios since they first came out – have built several. The Navy is looking for men like myself. I'd say my days here will soon be over."

Maybe it was pride at having a skill that was valued, or the fact that he had done her a good turn, or that he would soon be leaving his office job. But he looked like a different man. Taller. Confident.

"Well," he said, suddenly self-conscious. "See you on Monday." He spun around, grabbed his hat and coat from his desk, and left.

"Thank you, Mr. Weeble!" Lillian called out after him.

She went back to the switchboard room and slowly put on her hat and coat. The switchboard was dark, lifeless; the chairs empty. This was her last day there – she could hardly believe it. She stood a moment in the doorway, and felt an absurd rush of affection for the narrow, windowless room. A stepping stone, she said to herself, and left.

She walked to the elevator in a daze. How quickly everything had happened! She smiled to see that Izzy was there waiting for her.

"I couldn't help but overhear all the commotion," said Izzy. "Congratulations." She gave Lillian a quick hug, and they stepped into the elevator.

"Oh, Izzy. I just can't believe it! It was so unexpected. Did you have anything to do with this?"

"I'm afraid all the credit goes to Weeble. And to you, of course. Anyway, they're lucky to get you."

"I guess you were right about them both, Izzy. Though I have to say, it's Mr. Weeble who surprises me more."

"Maybe in time you'll change your mind about Mr. Rockwell."

"For your sake, I will, Izzy. If that's what you want."

Izzy waved away his name, as if Rockwell were nothing more than an annoying insect. She took Lillian's arm as they got off the elevator, and walked with her outside.

"Lilly, I'm really happy for you. And I want to say how sorry I am for the way I spoke to you. I've never spoken to anyone like that before. I've felt terrible ever since."

"It doesn't matter, Izzy. I just hate to see you so upset." They paused at the corner where Izzy usually turned to catch her bus. "Izzy, I know how hard it's been for you, with Red. But I'm sure things will work out."

"Always the optimist." Izzy frowned out at the traffic, then shook her head, and gave a wry laugh. She turned around and faced Lillian. "I got a letter. Last week."

"You mean from Red?"

Izzy nodded.

Lillian waited for her to say something more. "And?"

Izzy took a deep breath, and tried to sound matter-of-fact. "He married his nurse. Two months ago."

Lillian opened her mouth, her eyes searching Izzy's face. "I don't believe it," she whispered.

"It's true. Apparently she helped him get through a tough time. They were together a lot." Izzy shrugged, as if Lillian could guess the rest.

Lillian stood speechless. She couldn't think of anything to say that wouldn't sound trite, inadequate. "Oh, Izzy," was all she could say.

"I'll get over it. I'm slowly adjusting to the idea." She put her hands in her pockets and scanned the crowded street. "I think what I'm most angry about is that he waited to tell me. I've spent the last year worrying about the lout, and I've been in knots these past few months. I'm tired of it. I just want to put it behind me. Move on."

Everything fell into place for Lillian. Izzy's distance, her cold manner.

A softer expression came over Izzy's face. "The crazy thing is, sometimes I sit there, and I imagine him lying wounded, and depressed, sad about his buddies – and I'm actually thankful that there was a kind nurse there for him." She tried to make light of the situation that was breaking her heart. "And you know what a charmer Red can be." She pulled a hankie from her coat pocket and dabbed at her eyes and nose.

"Mr. Rockwell knows," continued Izzy. "Neither of us has any illusions about love or marriage. We're just happy to have someone to pass the time with. For now."

"Oh, Izzy. I'm so sorry. I should have known something was wrong."

Izzy gave another shrug. "We're at war, Lilly. This heartache of mine matters very little."

Lillian looked down, trying to make sense of everything. She put a hand on her friend's arm. "What are you going to do?"

"Do?" Izzy twisted her lips in thought and looked up at the sky. "I'm going to get a manicure." She brushed away the curls on her forehead. "Get this mop fixed. You've seen the ads, telling us that it's our duty to look beautiful for the men." Izzy did her best to imitate the glamorous movie stars in the ads: "Morale is a woman's business."

Lillian tried to smile, but she was deeply saddened, and worried for Izzy.

Izzy took Lillian's arm. "I'll be all right, Lilly. I never stay down for long. I've already wasted enough time. I don't want to waste any more. Life is too darned short."

*

All evening Lillian found herself thinking about Izzy and Red. She had always thought of them as such a happy couple. Now he was someone else's husband! It just didn't seem possible. Who knows, she thought. Maybe the same fate awaits me. It begins with a postponement, and then – She left her thought unfinished.

She wondered if Charles was keeping anything from her. She preferred the brutal truth to lies; at least with the truth, you were on firm ground, painful as it may be. Lies and half-truths were shifting ground that left you unable to think clearly.

She tried to imagine, once again, what had happened between her and Charles. It was unfair of him to make the decision about their wedding without discussing it with her. That's what most bothered her. If he simply wanted to wait a bit, she could understand that. But there was some reason he wasn't telling her. She was sure of it. Something made him think that it was his decision, and not hers. Maybe there was someone else he still thought about. She ran with that idea for a while, but kept coming up empty. He had never given her a moment's hesitation on that account. Or maybe he was just getting cold feet, afraid of having his life changed so dramatically. She could understand that as well. If that were the case, he should simply tell her. She would ask him directly the next time she saw him; not wait to find out months later, like poor Izzy.

After the boys went to bed, Lillian sorted through the mail. She noticed a letter from Annette and suddenly felt somewhat lifted. Here was an ally who would never desert her. The two sisters wrote to each other almost weekly, and Lillian always looked forward to her news. She sat on the couch, tucked her legs underneath her, and opened Annette's letter.

Annette wrote that Bernie was already at work on their vegetable garden, clearing and staking out a much larger garden to be planted in the spring. She wrote of their plans for Christmas, news from their town and how everyone was buying War Bonds, and how much the children missed Tommy and Gabriel. And then she wrote how sorry she was to hear that the wedding had been postponed.

I've been turning it over in my mind, and I'm afraid something I said might have influenced Charles. It was right after the news of the attack – I forgot I had even said it, until I received your letter saying that Charles wanted to wait on the wedding. Then I remembered. I told him how hard it was for you after Tom died. That you couldn't go through that again. That it took you so long to get over. I'm so sorry, Lillian. I should have known how Charles would take it. I guess I was just being the protective older sister. But after seeing you two together, and after getting to know him, I hope to God that you don't wait. You two belong together.

Lillian set the letter on her lap, and groaned as she thought of all the terrible things she had mentally accused Charles of. Because the postponement didn't make any sense, she had searched for, and come up with, any number of excuses: selfishness, fickleness, still being in love with someone else, not wanting to be tied down with a wife and children.

Yet she had never considered the one reason that did make sense: that he was sacrificing his own happiness for her sake.

# Chapter 13

For the last three days, Brendan had told himself to stop behaving like a foolish lad. To forget Mary Murphy, like he should have done long ago. The anger that had suffused him, slowly narrowed into a hounding desire to have an answer – any answer that would plug up the rush of sorrow and loss. He *would* have an answer. Even if it finally proved to him that she had simply never cared for him as he believed. He would see her one more time.

When Mrs. Murphy's bell rang, she knew it would be Brendan. She had been expecting him. Knew he would call on her one last time, to blame her or interrogate her, or simply to say goodbye. She was prepared.

"Come in, Brendan. Please, sit down. I'll make us a pot of tea."

"Don't bother. I'll not keep you long." He stood awkwardly near the door, twisting his cap in his hand.

When he didn't say anything more, she took him by the hand and led him to the couch. "Come. Sit down." She sat in the armchair next to the couch.

Mrs. Murphy almost smiled as Brendan launched right into what he had to say. He was never one for beating around the bush. He had always been straightforward and truthful. He spoke as if forty years did not sit between them.

"When you broke it off, I was angry, determined to stay away from you. I let a month go by, then when I couldn't stand it any longer, I went to your house and knocked on the door. Pounded, really," he said with a wry smile. "It was your sister who told me you had moved away. Why, it nearly broke my heart, and the sorrow was upon me, for I knew then that it was final. It was over.

"I buried myself in drink for a while, knowing how you would despise that. Then I exhausted myself traipsing all over the Northeast, working here and there. At some point, I realized that I was afraid of being alone. Afraid of being alone with my thoughts of you. The loss was more than I could bear.

"Elizabeth had been recently left at the altar. She was a proud woman and couldn't bear the thought that people would talk. She saw me look-ing hang-dogged at church, and began to con-vince me that we were a pair. Of course she meant that we had both been jilted, but I let her fool herself, and me, that we were well-suited. And so we married.

"The birth of Nancy kept us happy enough for a few years. But without anything ever being said, we gradually drifted apart. She became busy with the church, with Nancy. I let myself get lost in work. I think we both felt that we had failed each other. And ourselves."

Mrs. Murphy had not expected this. She had always imagined him happy, in his robust way of embracing life. Now, she realized how wrong she had been. She put a gentle hand on his arm, but he pulled back.

He shook away that part of his past, and made himself smile. "But our saving grace was Nancy. She made it all worthwhile. Forced me to think about someone besides myself. And, of course, now there's the grandchildren," he said, shifting to a strained cheerfulness. "All in all, life has been good."

He began twisting his hat in his hand again. "I didn't want you to think that I blamed you in any way, or held a grudge, or any bad feeling. We all have our reasons for doing what we do." He waited for her to say something, but she remained silent.

Again, he tried to smile, but his eyes showed sadness. He looked at the floor, and knitted his brows, as if seeing an old image there. "It's just that – I had imagined you so many times with some handsome fella, lots of kids – it took some doing to re-imagine things in my head."

Mrs. Murphy reached out to him again, and this time he let her take his hand.

"Mary," he said, only now looking up at her, "I'm glad our paths crossed again. I mean that. But – I need to know. Can you not tell me what happened? Can you not help me to make sense of it?"

The asking in his eyes nearly broke her heart. She knew that to let him go again, without the truth, would be a cruelty she was not capable of.

"Brendan," she began, forcing herself to look him in the eye. "I have been a coward. I am guilty of withholding the truth from you. Then. And now. I thought it was for the best. For both of us."

She waited for what seemed like several minutes before saying calmly, "I had cancer."

Her simple statement knocked the air out of him. He sat staring at her, trying to take in what she was saying.

"Breast cancer," she continued. "Uncommon for one so young, but not unheard of. They decided to take a radical approach." She gave him an airy smile. "I guess they made the right decision. I'm still here."

Brendan's stunned expression shifted as comprehension slowly pieced everything together. His eyes and mouth scrunched in slow, pained understanding. His eyes went from her face to her chest, back to her face.

She nodded.

He gave a short sound of pain, as if he had been struck a deep blow. "Ah, Mary," he said, embracing her tightly. Then he tossed his hat on the coffee table, and took her face in his hands. "Why did you not tell me? Did you think that would have changed anything?"

"I thought *I* would be different. We had such perfection. I couldn't bear the thought of becoming something else."

After several moments, Brendan sat back, squinting into the past. "I remember. You were tired. Those dark circles, the fatigue. I thought I had myself to blame for that. I thought I was demanding too much of your time and energy."

She rubbed his arm. "I should have told you. I was terrified myself. I didn't think I could handle your terror as well. I thought it would be easier, for me, to go through it alone. I didn't want anyone to know. I wanted to be able to pretend that I was the same. And it was easier to do so if I was on my own."

She gave him time for it to sink in. "It was the morning after our last night together – that I met with the doctor for the results. And he told me."

Brendan slowly shook his head. "I couldn't figure it out. When I asked you to marry me, and you accepted – that was the happiest day of my life. I went over and over that last night of ours. It all felt so right and true." He turned to her, seeing once again in detail, every moment of that day. "We walked along the river, Mary, do you remember?"

"Of course, I do."

"We strolled to that bench of ours, making plans. I'll never forget that kiss, not as long as I live." Then his smiled dropped to the floor, and he jerked back on the couch, as if he had just been struck with a sledgehammer. "Oh, Jaysus!" he cried, remembering the words he had spoken that night. He put his hands over his face and groaned. "I didn't know what I was saying. Oh, dear God, please don't tell me my words had any bearing on your decision!"

"No, Brendan, of course they didn't."

He held her and gently rocked, tears filling his eyes. Then again he held her face between his hands. "I would have said the same thing if it was your knee or your elbow or the small of your back I held in my hand."

"It wasn't your words, believe me, Brendan. It was me and my fear."

"To go through that alone. Oh, my poor dear girl. I should have been there for you." A glint of anger appeared in his eyes, and he dropped his hands onto his lap. "You had no right to take that away from me."

"I was young and proud and foolish. And scared. I didn't know how to handle it. I'm so sorry I caused you pain. I had hoped all these years that you were happy."

She watched him as he sat staring at the floor. She wanted to give him a graceful way out, and chose words that would minimize everything that had just passed between them. "I hope we can still be friends."

"*Friends?*" Brendan asked, surprised at the word. "Friends?" He leaned back, and wiped his eyes. "I don't think my heart will allow for that. I've never stopped loving you, Mary. Life has shaped me in a way that makes me love you more than ever."

He stood and took his hat. "My offer stands, till the day I die." He kissed her forehead, and quickly left.

# Chapter 14

Charles was relieved to see Mrs. Murphy back in the office. It was the 23$^{rd}$, and he wanted to see her before the Christmas holiday began. She had called in sick two days in a row – something she had never done in all the years she worked for him. Ever since his return from upstate, he had watched her stable personality fluctuate dramatically. First down, then up, then soaring, now down again. For the past two weeks or so, he had never seen her so happy – rushing out to lunch, leaving the office in a hurry, humming to herself. He had caught her smiling out at nothing on more than one occasion. She was like a young girl in love. But today she was once again subdued.

Charles and Mason took her out for a holiday lunch, and she put up a good front. They discussed their plans for Christmas, and the changes they would have to make in the office when they returned after the holidays.

"Three of our clerks are now with the Army," said Mason. "Several others have enlisted."

"We'll have to place an advertisement after the holiday," said Charles. "Lillian tells me to start hiring women. Promote and train the ones we have. Mason," he said, suddenly. "How about your sisters? They've all had training, haven't they? Do you think any of them would be interested in working with us?"

Mrs. Murphy clapped her hands. "What a wonderful idea, Mr. Drooms!" She turned to Mason excitedly. "What about your sister Edith? She's a typist, isn't she? Didn't you say she was looking for work?"

"Indeed, she is. And she has a head for numbers. I'll discuss it with her tonight." The idea obviously thrilled Mason, though he was trying his hardest not to show it.

"I hope she says yes," said Mrs. Murphy, perking up at the idea of being able to help the young woman. "Tell her I will personally take her under my wing." Mrs. Murphy smiled inwardly, remembering something Brendan used to say: The best way out of our own troubles, is to help someone else with theirs.

"Thank you, Mrs. Murphy. I'll be sure to tell her."

"I hope so, as well," said Charles. "I'd like to bring some good news to Lillian for a change. She would be delighted to know that I've acted on her suggestion."

Mrs. Murphy noticed the trace of sadness underneath his words.

When they returned to the office, Charles decided to close early. Everyone was eager to begin their Christmas vacation.

After the staff left, Mason said his goodbyes to Mrs. Murphy and Charles. "Merry Christmas to you both!"

Charles knew that Mason would hurry straight home and tell his sister the good news; it would make his whole family happy. Charles wished he had thought about hiring one of Mason's sisters earlier.

With the office to be closed for a week, Charles decided to speak to Mrs. Murphy before leaving. He wanted to make sure that she was all right. She looked well enough, but the earlier spark in her was definitely gone.

He stopped by her desk, on the pretext of giving her a folder.

"I guess we can wrap up and go home, Mrs. Murphy."

"I'm almost caught up. You go on ahead. I'll just finish with a few things and lock up." She placed the folder in the filing tray.

"Have you noticed the elevator operator lately?" Charles asked, trying to make small talk.

"Mr. Grimes?"

"He's taken to wearing his uniform from the Great War."

"Indeed, I've noticed," she chuckled. "I asked him about it, and he said it was his way of showing his support. I must say that his spirits have decidedly improved."

"Very likely that's where he got his limp," said Charles. "I guess we never really know why people behave the way they do, do we?"

Mrs. Murphy looked up at him, and then away, giving a noncommittal, "Hmm."

"Mrs. Murphy, I wanted to ask you – is everything all right? You're feeling well?"

"Yes, yes." She lifted the files out of the tray, and began to put them in alphabetical order.

Charles was unconvinced. He hated to interfere in a personal matter, but it was out of character for her to miss work, and to be so subdued. "You feel sufficiently recovered?"

"I'm well. Thank you, sir. It's – something else. My own fault…" She let her words trail off.

He stood there awkwardly, wondering how far to press her. "If you ever need time off or anything…"

"Truly, sir. I'm fine." She put on a cheerful face. "I'll be back to my old self in a couple of days."

"Well, good. I'm glad to hear it." He didn't want to pry any further, and began to leave.

"Sir?" she called out after him.

"Yes?" he said, turning around.

"What about you?"

Charles stood staring at her for a moment. "Me?"

"Yes. I've noticed that you have been downcast of late. Ever since you came back from your trip. Ever since you postponed your wedding, it seems to me. You haven't been yourself at all."

"I haven't?" He looked around, at the floor, the desk, wondering if this was true.

"No, indeed. You seem quite dejected. I wonder if you've made the right decision."

Charles tried to make light of the situation by giving a small laugh. "Well, I am disappointed to have to postpone it. Terribly. I can't deny it. But –"
He considered for a moment whether to confide in Mrs. Murphy. He didn't want to burden her with problems of his own, but he knew he could trust her, and that she would give sound advice.

"I was waiting to tell you after the holidays. I've already discussed it with Mason. I've re-enlisted. I'll be called to serve."

Mrs. Murphy nodded, and waited for more.

"It could be very soon," he added.

"And?" she asked, meeting his gaze.

"Well. Anything could happen, you know."

"And what exactly does that possibility have to do with your wedding?" She folded her hands, lifted her chin, and waited for an answer.

Charles felt like a schoolboy, caught in a flimsy excuse. Mrs. Murphy was fast becoming her old self, he thought. There was a take-charge tone in her voice that would not be naysaid.

"Well, I wouldn't want Lillian to suffer unnecessarily. She already lost one husband, you know. I wouldn't want her to go through that again."

Mrs. Murphy simply raised her eyebrows.

"And of course, there's always the chance that I could come back wounded. She's still so young."

"And she agrees with this reasoning?"

"Well, no. I mean, I haven't told her why I feel that we should wait."

"You've kept it to yourself? But surely that's a decision you have to make together as a couple," Mrs. Murphy said decisively. Then she blushed to hear her own words. Isn't that exactly what she had done to Brendan? Taken him out of the equation. She shook her head.

"Mr. Drooms, many years ago I made the same mistake, of making a decision for someone else, depriving them of a say in the matter. And I've had long years to regret it."

She looked up at him. "It really comes down to a simple yes or no question: Do you want to marry her?"

There was only one way to respond. "More than I've ever wanted anything in my life."

"Then listen to your heart, and don't let what might or might not happen get in your way!" Mrs. Murphy gave a light pound on the desk with her fist. "And for heaven's sake, discuss your worries with her. Talk it over. Listen to her."

Charles nodded, weighing her words. "I've been so torn, trying to decide what is best for her."

"She has a right to know. And it's wrong to let a chance for happiness pass you both by." Mrs. Murphy seemed to be considering her own words.

A smile slowly spread across his face. "You're absolutely right. I don't want to lose another moment."

"I'm glad to hear it! Life is too short." Mrs. Murphy was exactly like her old self now; no time for nonsense and dillydallying.

"Thank you for talking sense into my stubborn head. Goodnight, Mrs. Murphy. And Merry Christmas!"

"Good night, sir. And a very Merry Christmas – to both of you!" she laughed, and began to tidy up her desk for the day.

Charles reached for his coat and hat from the hall tree, and pulled on his coat. "Oh, Mrs. Murphy?" he asked before leaving.

"Yes, Mr. Drooms?"

He leaned around the corner and smiled. "I do hope you'll follow your own advice."

*

Lillian heard the reports that the Germans might launch an attack during Christmas week. The city, and the entire country, was on high alert. Lillian and the boys were off for Christmas week, and she wanted to keep them close to home, afraid to let them out of her sight. But Tommy and Gabriel kept asking to go outside with their friends. She couldn't blame them. She was busy in the kitchen, and this was Christmas week, after all. A time for play, and happiness, and celebration.

The day before, on her way home from work, Lillian had stopped by the library and picked up *The Count of Monte Cristo*. Gabriel was now begging Tommy to read it with him, but Tommy repeatedly refused.

"It's too long, Gabriel. It won't be any fun. Trust me."

Then Gabriel asked him to play games with him, checkers, Lincoln Logs, coloring.

"I don't want to read, or play checkers, or anything else. I want to go outside!" said Tommy.

"Gabriel," said Lillian from the kitchen. "I told you I would read the book to you."

"But I want Tommy to read it with me!"

Tommy heard whoops and cries from the street and ran to the window.

"Can't I go outside, Mom?" asked Tommy. "All the other kids are there."

"Yeah, Mommy," said Gabriel. "There's nothing to do inside."

Lillian felt like getting a breath of fresh air herself. "Well, I have to run to the store to get a few things. I'll walk out with you."

The boys ran to get their coats.

"But you have to stay on our street." Lillian pulled Tommy aside and spoke softly. "I want you to stay close, Tommy, just in case —"

"In case they bomb us. I know, I know, Mom. Don't worry. Me and Gabe know what to do."

The boys ran down the stairs and out the door, with Lillian trying to catch up to them. Tommy saw a group of boys outside of Mickey's brownstone, and ran to join them.

"I'll be right here, Mom," he called from the top step.

Lillian and Gabriel went to Mancetti's, and when she entered the store, she was surprised to see two policemen inside talking with an angry Mancetti.

"They've been at it for two weeks now!" Mancetti complained. "Throwing tomatoes and eggs, writing slurs. They're getting worse and worse, and nothing's being done about it!" He stood in his white butcher's apron, his arms crossed, waiting for an answer.

"Mr. Mancetti," began one of the policemen, "we've got our hands full. We've been keeping a lookout, but most likely it's just a bunch of boys who will soon get tired of their game and move on to something else."

Lillian quickly made her purchases. She wanted to get back and use the afternoon to make a few dishes for Christmas Day. As she was leaving, she saw that Mrs. Wilson had come in and was standing near the door, along with some other customers, trying to hear what all the commotion was with the policemen.

"Good afternoon, Mrs. Hapsey." Mrs. Wilson threw her arms up. "What's the world coming to? Threats from the sky above, hooligans on the ground. Harry's up on the roof all day, I'm running up and down to the air raid shelter. Goodness me!"

In spite of her words, Lillian thought that Mrs. Wilson seemed unusually happy. She was in her element being in charge of things, and Lillian had to admit that she excelled at it.

"Mrs. Hapsey, I *do* hope you'll stop by on Christmas Day. I've organized a sort of spotter's Christmas party. Harry has organized a platoon of men in our building. He's scheduled a twenty-four hour watch for the whole week." She shook her fist at the sky. "Just let them try. We're ready for them this time."

"Thank you, Mrs. Wilson. I'll be sure to stop by with the boys."

"Yes, it will be quite a time. Mrs. Kuntzman is helping with the baking, and will be with me most of the day."

"Mrs. Kuntzman?" Lillian asked, surprised at the tone of affection in Mrs. Wilson's voice.

"My staunchest ally. She's been supplying me with strudel and cherry krapfen for the spotters all week." She dropped her voice to add, "Though we've renamed them Yankee Cobbler and Allied Donuts. In the same way the restaurants have renamed spaghetti – Liberty Noodles, they call them.'"

"Yes, I've seen that," laughed Lillian.

"And she's promised one of her famous Christollens. Hmm. I'll have to come up with another name for it. Yes, Mrs. Kuntzman and I have been spending many of our evenings together, trading recipes, and helping out with Bundles for Bluejackets – knitting sweaters and caps for our men on the North Sea." Mrs. Wilson pulled Lillian closer and spoke confidentially. "She can out-bake me any day of the week, but my stitches are much tighter."

Lillian admired Mrs. Wilson's resolve. Domineering and sometimes overbearing, Mrs. Wilson was the kind of woman you wanted around in time of war. Capable, determined, unafraid. "I'll be sure to bring some Christmas cookies and gingerbread," said Lillian.

"Wonderful! And we'll have the radio on – listening to Mr. Lionel Barrymore read 'A Christmas Carol.' It should be quite a day." She leaned over to Gabriel. "And if the boys get bored with the women downstairs, they can run up to the roof and help the men spot enemy planes. Well, I won't keep you. Ta-ta!"

"Goodbye, Mrs. Wilson."

It would be a happy Christmas after all, thought Lillian. She would keep the boys busy all day, and it would be good for them to go out, to be with the neighbors. In just one year, this neighborhood had quickly turned into their new home, and she felt a deep love for the place and its people.

Outside the store, Lillian stopped to say hello to Mrs. Kinney, who was chatting with another neighbor. Just then, Gabriel spotted Tiny across the street, standing in the shadow of a doorway. He waved his cap once to catch Gabriel's attention.

Gabriel nodded at him and looked around. He was afraid the police were after Tiny.

Lillian and Gabriel walked back home with Mrs. Kinney and as they approached her brownstone, Lillian saw that Tommy and the other boys were gathered around a game of marbles.

"Goodbye, Mrs. Hapsey!" Mrs. Kinney called out, stepping around the group of boys.

"I'll be home in a little bit, Mommy," said Gabriel. "Don't worry. I'll stay on our street."

"Okay. Tommy, you'll keep an eye on Gabriel?"

"Sure," said Tommy, focused on the game.

Gabriel waited until she left, and then ran back to Tiny. He saw that Tiny's eyes were red and he was sniffling.

"Hi, Tiny. What's wrong? Did the police come?"

Tiny twisted his mouth, and rubbed his nose with his sleeve. "It's my brother. He – he died last night." Tiny swallowed. "He just couldn't hold on any longer. I told him, go ahead brother. Don't stay for me. You go and see Mom and Pop. Leave these old clothes behind you."

"Sorry, Tiny," said Gabriel. "I liked your brother."

"He liked you too, Gabriel."

Gabriel waited for Tiny to say something, but he just stood there, looking down.

"You can still talk to him though, right? Like you do with your mom?"

Tiny nodded. "I'll always be with my brother." He stood a little straighter. "Father Dwyer is – taking care of everything. He wants me to leave tonight – so that I can be at my uncle's in time for

Christmas. He sent a letter to my uncle this morning, to tell him about Marcel."

Gabriel watched Tiny's face. Now his friend would be all alone. "What are you going to do, Tiny?"

"Me?" Tiny stuffed his hands in his pockets. "I promised my brother that I'd go meet our uncle. So I'll go there. Say hey. See if he wants a nephew. If he doesn't, I'll go on and find that beach where we used to live. Learn how to fish or something. I might join the Army in a couple years. Figure I'd make a pretty good tail gunner. I got lots of plans."

"Will you still talk to me, too?" asked Gabriel.

"Sure, I will," said Tiny. "You made brother real happy with that toffee, Gabriel. It's like we had our old Christmas back, one last time. I'll never forget that." They began to walk down the sidewalk. "If you get a chance, come to the gazebo before dark. That was Marcel's favorite spot. I'm going to say my goodbye to him there. And then I'm going to leave."

"Okay, Tiny. I'll be there. I promise."

*

Just as the game of marbles finished, Butch and Platoon A ran up to Mickey and Tommy. "C'mon!" they whispered. "We need your help. We're on the trail of some spies."

"Confirmed spies," said Spider, smirking at Tommy.

"Nah," said Tommy, wanting to avoid Spider. "Maybe tomorrow."

"C'mon!" said Butch. "We have the enemy in sight." The boys ran off down the street.

Mickey jumped up to join them. "Let's go see what they've discovered."

Tommy reluctantly followed the group. But he held back when he saw them cross over to Mancetti's, fearing what the spiteful Spider had in mind.

Butch's gang huddled across from the store, with two boys positioned as look-outs. One of the boys took a tomato out of his pocket and threw it at the store window, while the gang cheered.

Tommy ran up and grabbed his arm. "Are you nuts? These are our neighbors!"

Spider and the other boys began to holler, "Dagos go home! Mussolini stinks! Dirty Wops! Go back where you came from!"

While Mickey and Tommy tried to break up the group, Tommy saw that Spider was reaching for something in his pocket. Before Tommy could get to him, Spider hurled a rock at the store window. It struck with a loud bang and the glass shattered. Screams came from inside.

"You dope!" cried Butch. "You always overdo it!" He and his gang took off running, scattering in different directions.

Mancetti ran out of the store waving a broom in the air, followed by the two policemen. A few customers ventured out, including Mrs. Wilson, and a crowd quickly gathered in front of the store.

Tommy had pounced on Spider before he could get away. They wrestled to the ground, rolling around on the sidewalk, arms and legs flailing. Tommy got in one satisfying punch at Spider's shoulder, but Spider quickly threw a fist at his nose. Tommy pulled back in pain, his eyes watering. He tasted blood and put his hand to his nose. Spider took the opportunity to scramble away.

Mancetti caught sight of Tommy, scowled, and lifted him by his arm. "I knew you were involved with that gang!"

Mrs. Wilson pulled his arm off Tommy. "Tommy had nothing to do with this. Can't you see they were attacking him, too?" She dug around in her purse and pulled out a hankie for Tommy.

Some of the onlookers also came to Tommy's defense. "It was those other boys. They ran off in that direction," said one of them.

"No, the one who threw the rock headed off that way. I saw him," said another.

The police started off in one direction, then in another, and then stood undecided about which way to turn. Just then, in the middle of all the confusion, Gabriel and Tiny walked up to the back of the crowd. When Mancetti saw Tiny, he pushed through the crowd and grabbed him by the collar.

"Here's the culprit! I've seen him hanging around, running off when he sees me."

"Leave him alone!" cried Gabriel. "He didn't do anything! He was with me."

Mrs. Mancetti came out of the store and yanked her husband's hand off of Tiny, and started arguing with him in Italian. Mancetti gestured with the broom, answering back in Italian, and pointing to Tiny and the broken window.

The two policemen stepped forward. "In English!"

"I tell him this is good boy," said Mrs. Mancetti. "This is Tiny. He help me. He wash off bad words those boys write. I give him food."

Tommy's eyes popped open and he nearly choked. "TINY?"

Mancetti folded his arms. "So you're the little thief who's been taking our food."

"Oh, for heaven's sake!" said Mrs. Wilson, throwing her arms up.

"No thief!" cried Mrs. Mancetti, standing in front of Tiny. "Tiny good boy. He work for his money. His brother is sick."

Tiny whispered to Gabriel. "I have to make a run for it. If they lock me up I'll never get away." He twisted through the crowd, dodging arms, and ducking, and then, fast as lightning, he disappeared around the corner.

"Run, Tiny!" yelled Gabriel. "Run!"

Mrs. Wilson had stepped aside to give the boy a clear path and planted herself in front of Mancetti just as he tried to make a swipe at Tiny. She and Mancetti then moved left and right, trying to get out of each other's way, which allowed Tiny a few extra seconds for his escape.

"Run!" cried Gabriel.

"Catch that thief!" Mancetti hollered to the policemen.

"He no thief, I say!" cried Mrs. Mancetti. She took the broom away from her husband and threw it on the ground, and started in Italian again, leaving the policemen unsure of what to do.

One of the policemen bent over and spoke to Gabriel. "Now, who's this Tiny lad? Did he throw the rock?"

"No! He's my friend. He was with me. He didn't throw anything."

Tommy ran up. "Gabriel!" he cried, putting an arm around his shoulder, and turning to the policemen. "This is my brother —"

The older policeman ignored Tommy, and spoke to Gabriel. "Do you know where this Tiny fella lives?"

Gabriel nodded. "His brother just died there. So Tiny's going to the warm place."

"You're saying there's a body there?" asked the younger policeman.

"I guess so – I don't know," Gabriel started to explain, but the older policemen leaned down close to Gabriel.

"The lad was just here. Now how could he already be going to a warm place? Are you sure you're not pulling our leg?"

"Yes," said Gabriel. "I mean, no. I mean –"

"Let's go and talk to the lad's parents," said the policeman.

"They don't have any parents," said Gabriel.

The older policeman sighed, pushed his hat back, and nudged the other. "We better look into this."

"What about my window?" asked Mancetti.

"Oh, for *goodness'* sake!" said Mrs. Wilson, rolling her head in disbelief.

"We're trying to get to the bottom of this," said the older policeman. "We'll go find the scamp and sort this all out."

The policeman put his hands on his knees and leaned down again to Gabriel. "Now, can you show us where he lives?"

Tommy appeared horrified at the idea of the police taking Gabriel away. He put both arms around him securely. "You can't take him away. My mom won't like that."

"We'll be right back. Come on, son. Step into the car."

Tommy looked on in fear as the policeman drove off with Gabriel. He was about to run home, but Mancetti grabbed him by his collar.

"Oh, no you don't! Now. From the beginning," said Mancetti. "I want to know who threw that rock, and why you were with those boys."

Tommy began to tell him exactly what had happened, with details added by some of the bystanders, and a fierce defense by Mrs. Wilson.

Still unsatisfied, Mancetti asked Mickey to tell his version. After several minutes of questioning the boys, Mancetti was finally convinced that Tommy had nothing to do with the broken window. He relented and placed a hand on Tommy's shoulder. "All right then. You'd better go and get your mother."

*

Lillian had her door cracked open, waiting for Tommy and Gabriel. She heard the vestibule door open and quick footsteps coming up the stairs. She opened her door, glad that they were back so soon. She was surprised to see Charles running up the last flight of stairs. He was a good two hours earlier than she had expected.

"Charles! You're home early?"

He threw his arms around Lillian. "I couldn't wait. I had to see you."

Lillian stepped back to look at him, wondering at the change in him. "Come in. I want to talk to you, too." She closed the door behind him.

He was impatient and grabbed both of her hands. "Lillian. I don't want to postpone the wedding. I never did. It's just that –"

"It was my sister, wasn't it? I had a letter from her. Really, Charles, you should have discussed it with me!"

"I know, I know. I just – started to imagine all sorts of things. That I could come home injured, or not at all."

Lillian put a hand on her hip. "And what if I get sick or injured while you're away? Does that mean you'll change your mind about me?"

He laughed and embraced her. "Of course not! Nothing would ever make me change my mind about you. I want to be married to you more than anything else in the world. I don't want to wait."

Lillian's face flooded with hopefulness. "You mean – we can get married in May?"

"We can get married tomorrow if you want!"

Lillian threw her arms around him, overjoyed at the thought of marrying him soon, and that nothing had changed between them.

"Mom!" came Tommy's urgent cry.

Lillian and Charles broke apart, and stared at each other as they listened. They heard the vestibule door close and someone running up the stairs.

"Mom!"

Just as Lillian opened the door again, Tommy burst through, blood under his nose and on his shirt. "Mom! The police!"

"Tommy!" she said, alarmed. "Are you all right?"

She saw the blood under his nose and ran to get a wet washcloth.

Tommy leaned over, trying to catch his breath. "Not me," he panted. "The police –"

She started to place the washcloth to his nose, but he pushed her arm away. "The police have Gabriel!"

"What?" Lillian started back in horror. "Is he hurt? What happened? Where is he?"

"He's – he's fine." Tommy leaned against the wall, still panting. "Gabriel was telling the truth, Mom. There really is a Tiny!"

Lillian's mouth dropped open. "What?"

Charles placed a hand on Tommy's shoulder. "Tell us what happened, Tommy."

"We were playing marbles and then Butch came and said they found some spies and we followed them to Mancetti's, and then Spider threw a rock and broke the window and Mr. Mancetti thought Tiny did it, so Tiny ran away, and Gabriel is taking the police to Tiny's home to see if there's a body there because his brother just died and they need Gabriel to show them where he lives!"

Lillian didn't need to hear anything else. She rushed down the stairs, out the building, and ran all the way to Mancetti's, followed by Charles and Tommy.

"Gabriel? Where's Gabriel?" Lillian scanned the crowd that was still gathered outside the broken window. She ran to Mrs. Mancetti. "Where's Gabriel?"

"Police take him. He say Tiny's brother dead." She made the sign of the cross. "Gabriel show them where he live." She looked at her husband, and huffed. "Tiny good boy!"

Lillian saw Mancetti in the middle of the crowd and pushed her way through to him. "Mr. Mancetti?"

He knew he had been wrong, so his only response was, "Who's going to pay for my window?"

Lillian faltered, and Charles pulled her onto the bench. He took off his coat and draped it around her shoulders. She had run out without a coat and was now shivering.

Mrs. Wilson sat down next to her and began her account of what happened, but Mancetti cut in and wanted to start at the beginning with the graffiti, and how business was slowing down because of the young hoodlums causing trouble, throwing tomatoes, and now rocks.

Just then, the police car pulled up. When Gabriel climbed out with one of the policemen, Lillian ran over and held him tightly.

"Are you all right, Gabriel?" She took him to the bench and pulled him onto her lap and kissed his head. "My darling boy. What – what happened?" She looked to the policemen, then to Gabriel for an explanation, then over at Tommy.

They all began to explain as best they could: the two policemen, Mr. and Mrs. Mancetti, Tommy, Mrs. Wilson, Gabriel, Mickey, and some of the onlookers, adding details, picking up different threads of the story, and talking over each other. Lillian and Charles turned from one person to another, trying to piece everything together, but were unable to make sense of the string of words: gang of boys, Mata Hari, broken window, warm beaches, Platoon A, Spider, braunschweiger, Father Dwyer, police, Marcel, Tiny...

Lillian took Gabriel's face in her hands. "Gabriel! Why didn't you tell me that Tiny was a real boy?"

"I did tell you, Mommy."

Lillian looked to Charles, then back to Gabriel, wondering exactly why she hadn't believed him.

The policemen examined the window while Mancetti swept up the glass. Mrs. Mancetti went back inside to tend to the shoppers lined up to make their purchases, now that the drama was over.

Lillian and Charles walked home with the boys, Lillian's mind scattering in a hundred directions. Tommy and Gabriel walked ahead of them.

Tommy draped his arm around Gabriel. "Sorry I didn't believe you, Gabe."

"I got to sit in the front seat, Tommy. Did you see that?"

"I sure did."

"And they showed me how the police radio works."

When they reached their apartment, Lillian took off Gabriel's coat and kissed his head. She then sat with him on the couch, holding him tightly. Tommy sat on her other side and she wrapped her arms around both of them.

After a moment, Tommy ran to his bedroom, and came back holding something behind his back.

"I was saving it for you for Christmas. How about we read it tonight?" He held up a Classic Comics version of *The Count of Monte Cristo*. "Better than the book. This is shorter, and has lots of pictures. Look!" he said, handing it to Gabriel.

"Thanks, brother!" said Gabriel, jumping up and hugging Tommy around the waist. He started to flip through the comic book.

Lillian and Charles went to the kitchen and sat at the table. Charles spoke softly. "I'll speak with Father Dwyer tomorrow. Find out more about the boy, see what we can do for him."

"Were they really living all alone? Sick and in poverty?" asked Lillian.

"Apparently so," said Charles.

Lillian gazed down at the table, her mind filled with visions of taking care of the boy. Cooking warm meals for him and buying him new clothes until they could locate his family. Or perhaps even bringing him into their home. She looked up at the window and saw that the day was starting to darken. She shook her head and sighed. "I'll get dinner started."

Gabriel walked into the kitchen; he had put his coat back on.

"Gabriel?" asked Lillian. She didn't know what to expect from him anymore.

"Don't be mad, Mom, but I have to go and say goodbye to Tiny. He's going to leave for the warm place. He's waiting for me at the park. I have to hurry."

"I don't want to let you out of my sight!" said Lillian.

"But, Mommy, I promised! I have to go!"

"I'll go with him," said Charles. "We'll be back before dinner. I promise."

Tommy started to grab his coat.

"You're not going anywhere, young man!" said Lillian, not quite sure how Tommy figured into everything, but knowing that he hadn't been watching Gabriel as closely as she had believed.

After Charles and Gabriel left, Tommy walked into the kitchen, and without being told, he began to set the table.

"Sorry, Mom. I didn't know. Don't be mad at me."

Lillian put her arms around him. "I'm not mad at you, sweetheart. I should have been more careful." She had been so concerned with harm coming from the sky, that she hadn't considered danger from other places.

"Gabriel could have been hurt or something," said Tommy. "And it would have been all my fault."

Tommy was so rarely downcast, that Lillian gave him a quick squeeze to cheer him up. "How about we have our gingerbread tonight? Will you help me whip the cream?"

"Sure!" said Tommy, perking up. "That'll make Gabriel happy."

*

On the way to the park, Gabriel told Charles all about Tiny and his brother, the orphanage and the nuns, and how Tiny was going to the warm place to meet his uncle, and collect shells and eat coconuts.

The lights in the park were just twinkling on as Charles and Gabriel walked over to the gazebo by the lake. Charles doubted that the boy would show up, but he wanted to do anything that would put Gabriel's mind at ease. They took a seat inside the gazebo and waited.

After a few moments Gabriel jumped up. "I know where he is," he said, and he walked down to the lake.

Charles followed him, and there in the gloaming, he saw a figure gazing out at the darkening water, his thin shoulders showing the quiver of restrained weeping.

Tiny heard a noise and whipped around, his eyes full of fear.

"It's okay, Tiny," Gabriel called out. "It's just me and –" Gabriel turned to Charles. "Are you still going to be my dad?"

"Of course, I am," said Charles, surprised that Gabriel was in any doubt.

"It's just me and Mr. Drooms, who's gonna be my dad. It's okay."

Charles stepped forward and took a closer look at what he first thought was a little boy. The person now seemed much older, wizened, worn – though he must be only thirteen or so. He was thin, his clothes tattered. There was a youthful energy about him, but his face was old with sadness and worry. A boy-man, just as Gabriel had described him.

"Hey, Tiny." Gabriel ran over and stood next to his friend.

"Hiya, Gabriel." He glanced over at Charles.

"I went to your place with the police. But everything was already gone."

"I have all my stuff," Tiny said.

They stood in silence for a few moments.

Tiny gazed out at the black lake. A few shimmering lights reflected on its surface, and when the breeze ruffled the water it looked like a sudden sprinkling of stars had just been cast from the heavens. Tiny reached for something inside his jacket, and in one fluid movement he tossed an old tattered book out into the dark water.

"Goodbye, Marcel," he said softly. "Goodbye, my brother."

Gabriel looked up at Tiny. "*The Count of Monte Cristo*?"

Tiny nodded. He looked out at the spot where the book had sunk, and watched the glittering ripples widen and fade. Then a subtle shift slowly took place on his face. The corners of his mouth lifted; the weariness faded, and youthfulness brightened his eyes. "He's making his escape now." He turned to Gabriel and smiled.

Tiny looked back out over the lake, and then raised his eyes up to the starry sky. After a few moments, he walked back to the gazebo. From under the bench, he picked up his old black bag, and slung it over his shoulder.

Charles's heart went out to the small figure. "Tiny," he said. "Where exactly are you going?"

"To my uncle's. And then to the warm place."

"Could you wait a day? And leave tomorrow?" Charles wanted to speak to Father Dwyer first, and get a warm meal inside the boy, and make sure he was prepared for his journey.

"I have to leave tonight so that I'm there by Christmas."

Charles hesitated before asking, "How are you going to get there?"

"My bus ticket will get me to my uncle's. After that, I guess I'll walk."

Charles started to reach for his wallet, but Tiny took a step back, and looked askance at him.

"I would like to help with the bus fare, Tiny."

Tiny put his hands behind his back. "No, thank you."

"Tiny earns his own keep," explained Gabriel.

Charles didn't want to offend the boy's pride, but he wanted to make sure he would have enough for food until he arrived. "I would want someone to help Gabriel, if he were in your place."

Tiny wasn't convinced.

"It's okay, Tiny," said Gabriel. "I had a dream that your mom said it was okay. She said, 'thank you for helping my darling boy.'"

Tiny swallowed and his eyes momentarily shone with happiness. "You did? No fooling, Gabriel?"

"No fooling. She said you should do it for your brother."

"My brother?"

"Yep."

Charles folded all the bills he had in his wallet and put them in Tiny's coat pocket, and then offered his hand.

Tiny shook his hand, and then bent down to make an adjustment to his shoe, roughly wiping his eyes and nose with his sleeve.

He stood back up, and took a deep breath. "Well, I better go now." He turned to Gabriel. "Bye, Gabriel."

"Thanks for being my friend, Tiny," said Gabriel. "I never had a best friend before."

Tiny gave a small embarrassed laugh, and gave Gabriel a quick hug, and a nod to Charles. He gave one last look behind him at the lake, and then oriented himself towards the future. "Well, so long then."

"So long, Tiny." Gabriel watched his friend walk away. The small dark figure was briefly illuminated as he passed under the lamp light, and then he blended with the darkness.

Charles's brow knitted in worry as he watched Tiny's departure. Then he put his arm around Gabriel, and they walked in the other direction, towards home.

"Did you really have that dream, Gabriel?"

"Well, somebody made me think those words. Maybe it was his mom."

Charles took his hand. "Come on. I bet dinner's already on the table."

They walked in silence a while, Charles worrying that Gabriel was too young to be exposed to the realities of poverty, illness, and death. He looked down at him.

"What are you thinking about, Gabriel?"

"*Dumbo*."

"*Dumbo*?" laughed Charles.

"Yeah," he smiled. "Remember when Dumbo and the mouse were asleep in the tree? And then they fell in the water and woke up?" He lifted his face to Charles. "Think we can we see it again?"

Charles put an arm around Gabriel's shoulder. "Sure, we can."

\*

Mrs. Murphy decided on a tiny bit of lipstick as she looked at herself in the mirror. She was dressed in her holiday red coat and hat. After Brendan left the other night, she sat for a long time remembering her younger, fearful self. She replayed that last night with Brendan in Boston. And the follow-up appointment with her doctor the next day: shock at his diagnosis, horror at his remedy. He had said there was no other way. That night, she had bravely stood before the mirror, parted her robe, and said goodbye to her body; goodbye to her dreams of love with Brendan. Those were dreams that would now belong to some other woman, some healthy woman with a future.

Well, she thought, as she dabbed on the lipstick, she now lived in that future. She had survived. She had been wrong to take away Brendan's choice in the matter. She took the locket from inside her blouse and draped it on the outside. Your heart has been hidden for too long, she told herself.

She headed back to the department store, rode the escalator to the fifth floor, and made her way to the North Pole. There was Brendan in his final act for the season, doing his best to come across as a jolly Santa, but it was a subdued performance. When he finished up with the last of the children, Mrs. Murphy stepped up to the stage.

His face flashed with joy when he saw his Mary Margaret standing there in front of him. He took off his Santa hat, and came down the stairs to greet her. When he saw the locket, tears filled his eyes. "You kept it then? All these years?"

"I've never taken it off."

Brendan was afraid to speak, afraid to ask why she had come. They walked together down the escalator, and through the store. He kept looking at her, and couldn't help but notice how happy she appeared. She seemed years younger, just like the girl he had known. But he didn't want to allow his hopes to rise.

They left the department store, and after a few steps, Brendan stopped and faced her. He waited for her to answer the asking in his eyes.

Mrs. Murphy smiled, linked her arm in his, and continued walking. "Would you care to be having dinner with me?" she asked. "I know of a little place. A fine Irish pub not far from here. I thought we could discuss our plans for Christmas."

Brendan let his face fill with hope. There was his sweet girl smiling up at him. Surely it could mean only one thing.

"What are you saying, Mary Margaret – what does this mean?"

Mrs. Murphy laughed and took his hands. "Quite simply, that there's life to be lived!"

A few last minute shoppers and workers rushing home couldn't help but notice the striking older couple walking arm in arm, both dressed in red, and clearly in love. The children who passed them believed they were seeing Mrs. Claus with Santa, and tugged on their parents' hands to stop – then stood open-mouthed and wide-eyed when, in the middle of the bustling, crowded sidewalk, the couple in red stopped, embraced, and kissed.